D0430940

The House of Djinn

Also by Suzanne Fisher Staples

Shabanu: Daughter of the Wind

Haveli

Suzanne Fisher Staples

EMBER

This is a work of fiction. Names, characters, places, and incidents either are the product of the author's imagination or are used fictitiously. Any resemblance to actual persons, living or dead, events, or locales is entirely coincidental.

Text copyright © 2008 by Suzanne Fisher Staples
Cover photograph copyright © 2012 by michaeljung/Shutterstock

All rights reserved. Published in the United States by Ember, an imprint of Random House Children's Books, a division of Random House, Inc., New York. Originally published in hardcover in the United States by Farrar, Straus and Giroux, LLC, New York, in 2008. Published by arrangement with Farrar, Straus and Giroux, LLC.

Ember and the E colophon are registered trademarks of Random House, Inc.

The lines of poetry on page 7 were taken from *These Branching Moments: Forty Odes by Jelaluddin Rumi,* translated by John Moyne and Coleman Barks, published by Copper Beech Press.

Visit us on the Web! randomhouse.com/teens

Educators and librarians, for a variety of teaching tools, visit us at randomhouse.com/teachers

The Library of Congress has cataloged the hardcover edition of this work as follows:
Staples, Suzanne Fisher.
The house of djinn / Suzanne Fisher Staples.—1st ed.
p. cm.
Summary: An unexpected death brings Shabanu's daughter, Mumtaz, and nephew, Jameel, both aged fifteen, to the forefront of an attempt to modernize Pakistan, but the teens must both sacrifice their own dreams if they are to meet family and tribal expectations.
ISBN 978-0-374-39936-8
[1. Family life—Pakistan—Fiction. 2. Sex role—Fiction. 3. Spirits—Fiction. 4. Pakistan—Fiction.] I. Title.
PZ7.S79346Hou 2010
[Fic]—dc22
2007005093

ISBN 978-0-307-97642-0 (pbk.)

RL: 6.5

Printed in the United States of America

10 9 8 7 6 5

First Ember Edition 2012

Random House Children's Books supports the First Amendment and celebrates the right to read.

In memory of Mona Megalli,
the world's best traveling companion
1958–2007

The House of Djinn

Author's Note

The story of the many peoples of the land we know as Pakistan is one of the oldest stories on earth, even though the nation itself is only sixty years old. The land was settled, conquered, and resettled by Indo-Aryans, Persians, Greeks, Arabs, and Afghans; by Hindus, Muslims, and Buddhists; and finally by the British, who ruled Pakistan as part of colonial India for almost one hundred years. Together, these peoples contributed to the development of Pakistan as a culturally diverse land.

In 1947 the British departed, leaving behind the independent states of India and Pakistan. Pakistan was founded on the principles of law that govern Britain and the United States, but in parts of the country tribal law prevails. The tribes of the four provinces—Sindh, Baluchistan, Punjab, and the North-West Frontier—include large groups such as the Pashtun in the northwest, and other clans that have exerted political influence since 1947.

Many tribal leaders, or sardars, are members of the provincial and national assemblies, and others have served at the highest levels of government. Wealthy sardars keep houses in the national capital at Islamabad or in the provincial capitals where they live when government is in session, or where they run family businesses.

Lahore, where this story takes place, is the capital of Punjab Province. It was one of the seats of power for the Mughal emperors, who ruled the vast lands of the Indian subcontinent for more than two hundred years. Lahore remains the most beautiful, cultured, and interesting city in Pakistan today, with many of its treasures preserved as historical monuments. Still, Punjabi tribal leaders regularly return home to arid, dusty places that are the seats of their tribal lands.

While tribal leadership is usually hereditary, sometimes a ruling sardar will overlook his eldest son in favor of another son or nephew who for one reason or another is more suitable as a leader. The sons of modern tribal leaders—and with increasing frequency their daughters—are often educated abroad, but many return home to assume tribal duties when their families need them.

The language spoken by the fictional Amirzai family and other characters in this story would most likely be Punjabi or Urdu, liberally sprinkled with English, especially idiomatic English. The glossary contains mostly Urdu words, many of Arabic, Persian, or Hindi origin.

Marriages in Pakistan are traditionally arranged. In tribal families, when business and political interests are at stake, a sense of familial duty may override any objection the bride and groom have to the match on personal grounds. But the personal preferences of the young man and woman are frequently taken into account by parents whose primary interest is in seeing that their son or daughter is happily married with a secure financial future.

The House of Djinn draws on tribal traditions to create a world that is typical of some families of Pakistani tribal leaders, and not at all typical of others. The patriarch of the fictional Amirzai family is very modern and forward-looking, as some (but not all) sardars are. As in most families, personalities clash, people reconcile, and some go their separate ways. And as in most families—both real and fictional—love is a powerful force that draws imperfect people together in the face of jealousy, greed, and the demands of tradition.

1

A small, slender woman with dark eyes stood near the edge of the roof looking out over the walled city of Lahore and reimagined her life. She had watched the seasons change over the red sandstone walls and the marble domes of the Badshahi Mosque for ten years. But this day she'd awakened knowing it would be the last morning of her old life.

Behind her, pigeons burbled and cooed softly to each other as they settled onto their roosts inside a room-sized wire cage in the middle of the rooftop courtyard. She let herself into the enclosure and picked up one of the birds, Barra, a proud old male who nestled his beak into the crack between her fingers.

The birds had belonged to Rahim, Shabanu's husband. After he was gone they were hers. In the old days, when the telephone trunk lines were undependable, Rahim had kept the pigeons to send messages back to his farm in Okurabad, about two hundred miles away. His most trusted servant,

Ibne, kept another set of pigeons at the farm to return messages to the haveli in the city. Pigeons fly home with unfailing instinct, but they will not fly in the opposite direction. And so Ibne and Rahim transported the birds back and forth by truck. Later, when the telephone trunk lines were replaced by satellite signals, Rahim and Ibne continued to use the birds. They never tired of talking about them, comparing their speed and the color of their feathers: green for faithfulness, gray for speed, brown for strength.

Shabanu handled them every day when she fed them and changed their water and cleaned their cages. She stroked Barra's round gray head with the knuckle of her forefinger. The pigeon turned a pink eye on Shabanu, and his tiny heart fluttered against the palm of her hand.

Shabanu imagined words that might let her family know she was alive and well, that she would come to them soon. They must be words that would not expose herself and her daughter, Mumtaz, to her murderous brother-in-law Nazir. They must be beautiful words that would speak to her parents' hearts. Even as she contemplated the danger of sending them, she knew what they would be.

She stroked Barra's breast again and pressed her lips to feathers that shone pink and gray and green all at once before releasing him back into the enclosure. She shut the door to the cage behind her and walked past the parapet that overlooked the mosque and the Shahi Qila, the Old Fort adjacent to it.

Every day of her ten years on the roof of the haveli Shabanu had looked out at the fort and thought of Anarkali, who had been buried alive inside its western wall at the turn of the seventeenth century. The Mogul emperor Akbar had murdered the beautiful dancing girl whose name meant "pomegranate blossom" because his son had fallen in love with her.

When Shabanu had awakened this morning, her first thought was this: "You are living like the dead." Nothing had changed. She knew Nazir would kill her if he found her, just as he'd threatened to do after he'd killed his brother Rahim, and Shabanu had refused to marry him. But this morning she awoke knowing Nazir no longer had power over her. She tried to connect this thought to a dream, or a conversation she might have overheard from one of the rooftops across the way. But it felt more like a notion that had been swimming below the surface, circling like a primitive fish toward the light, waggling at her insistently, as if warning her not to ignore it.

Every night, from the realm of the buried, Shabanu dreamed of Mumtaz asking a child's questions, about where the stars went during the day, and why the shadow of the sun followed her wherever she went. There had been no one to answer these wonderings as her daughter grew. Now Mumtaz was fifteen, a young woman, and Shabanu imagined her with narrowed eyes that accused her mother of betrayal when she learned Shabanu had hidden herself away all these years. The heat of shame in Shabanu's cheeks was the most familiar sensation she felt when she thought of her daughter.

These ten years Shabanu had felt the absence of Mumtaz

more keenly than she'd ever felt her presence. It was like a piece missing from the center of her heart where a mother's love should be.

The other greatest source of Shabanu's pain was that she'd left her mother and father growing old in the Cholistan Desert believing she was dead. She wanted to go to them, to ease their hearts, to see for herself that they were well. Sometimes it seemed her heart was made more of holes than solid parts, and that was her reason for sending the pigeon to Ibne. She had a physical need to see her daughter and to return to Cholistan.

Her days on the rooftop of the haveli were not so bad. Rahim's sister, Selma, who lived in the great old house below, visited her every day. Often they played cards in the evening, and talked over dinner. Samiya, a widow who was Selma's house servant and companion, joined them when she'd finished her chores in the kitchen.

Shabanu dreamed of a future in which she would return to Cholistan and teach the desert women to read so they could teach their children. She studied and she wrote poems and played her flute on the roof of the haveli, which stood a half story taller than the surrounding houses, so no one ever saw her. The poems were the letters from her heart that she couldn't send because no one could know she was alive. The flute music was her conversation with the world, expressing all of the wonder and hope she felt, despite her limited life.

Shabanu entered the summer pavilion, whose walls of carved marble screens had been her prison and her home.

She crossed the stone-tiled floor to the low wooden desk where she had learned to read, and where she wrote and studied. Samiya had taught Shabanu and Mumtaz to read and write, first in Urdu and then in English. Shabanu sat on the floor cushion behind the desk and picked up the pen from the slot in its surface. She drew a sheet of the lightest parchment from the desk drawer and remembered the lines of a poem by the Sufi mystic Rumi. She wrote:

> *Flying toward thankfulness you become*
> *the rare bird with one wing made of fear,*
> *and one of hope.*

She folded the parchment, and refolded it into a square, then rolled it into a thin cylinder. She stood and returned to the pigeon enclosure. She closed the door and held out her hand. Barra landed lightly on her wrist. Shabanu talked softly to the bird and flicked the latch on the plastic capsule attached to Barra's leg. The lid clicked open. She threaded the parchment into the compartment and snapped the lid back into place. She stroked the pigeon's cheek once more and carried him to the edge of the roof.

Reaching both hands toward the sky, she released Barra. Immediately the bird's wings stroked the air, and he rose up against the red walls of the Shahi Qila. Shabanu's heart lifted as the pigeon, who'd been imprisoned on the haveli's roof for the same ten years, dipped, then soared as he caught the wind, his wings golden-edged in the sharpening light of morning. The last Shabanu saw of Barra was the iridescent green flash of his neck feathers as he rose against the red wall where Anarkali remained buried to that day.

Barra was an old bird, and had not flown any distance in a very long time. But he had been one of Rahim's best pigeons, and Shabanu believed he would fly for his home at Okurabad, faithful and mindless as an old retainer. Ibne would be there to open his cage. He would recognize Barra, and from the poem he'd know that only Shabanu could have sent him. Ibne and Rahim had shared a love of the Sufi poets, especially Rumi. Every evening one of them would recite a Rumi poem, and the other would reply with another. Shabanu learned them by heart before she could read.

Rahim had fallen in love with Shabanu when she was only a girl. She was on a ladder rescuing her cousins from a tree when he saw her first, and he was captivated by her flashing eyes. He'd never stopped loving her, although her family were poor, nomadic camel herders. Rahim sent Ibne as a go-between, bearing gifts of gems in small lambskin sacks for Shabanu and her family. Ibne rode into the desert on a handsome white stallion, and he spoke to her parents with respect. Shabanu never loved Rahim and never wanted to marry him. But her parents had left her no choice, and he had been a good husband. She was certain Ibne would carry her note and read it to her parents in the Cholistan Desert.

Shabanu gazed at the sky beyond the minaret until long after Barra disappeared. And then she began to plan the rest of her day. Selma was going to visit her brother Mahsood, who had succeeded Rahim as tribal leader, for the afternoon and evening. Mahsood lived in a rambling old colonial bungalow across the city in Gulberg. Rahim always said his brother's house was haunted by mischievous djinn spirits: strange smells emanated from its interior, and lights appeared from nowhere, hovering menacingly before disappearing again. Rahim had seldom gone there. It was the house where Mumtaz lived, and Shabanu could bear the thought only because Rahim's nephew Omar also lived there, and she trusted him to protect her daughter with his life.

Selma wouldn't return until after a big dinner in honor of her niece Nargis and her family, who were returning to San Francisco after spending the summer in Lahore.

On this first day of her new life, Shabanu planned to slip out of the haveli while Selma was away and Samiya was busy, first in the laundry and then with shopping for groceries. Selma and Samiya were the only two people on earth who knew Shabanu lived on the roof. They had protected Shabanu faithfully these ten years, because they knew how dangerous Nazir could be.

Today Shabanu would hide herself within the billowing folds of a burqa and walk deeper into the old city to the bazaar, just to see what life looked like, this life that had been slipping past without her.

Shabanu waited inside the pavilion when she heard Samiya's quick knock at the door at the top of the stairs from the center courtyard below.

"I think the sky will turn itself inside out this morning," Samiya said. "I'm going to hurry with the laundry. Perhaps it'll dry before it rains." She set Shabanu's breakfast tray down on the table and poured tea. A glass of sweet lime juice, cloudy green and fragrant, and a plate with two onion paratha sat on the tray. "Would you like anything else?" Shabanu shook her head and smiled, and Samiya scurried out of the room, collecting Shabanu's dirty laundry from the basket at the back wall, outside the bathroom, as she went.

Samiya was just a few years older than Shabanu. She had worked as an ayah in the haveli across the lane. When the children were grown, Samiya had moved into Selma's house. She and Shabanu had become fast friends. Shabanu loved Samiya's birdlike quickness, her efficiency of movement and thought, her absolute loyalty, her sense of fun.

Shabanu heard the rhythmic thump of the washing machine down in the courtyard. She went to the trunk in her wardrobe and dug deep down to the bottom until she found the voluminous gray burqa that she hadn't worn since she took up life on the roof of the haveli. It smelled of mold and mothballs. Shabanu shook it out and laid it across her bed.

She imagined Samiya pulling the white sheets through the wringer that sat on the rim of the washing machine's tub, the sleeves of her tunic rolled above her elbows.

Shabanu took a deep breath and slipped the burqa over her head, adjusting it so the embroidered square through which she could barely see was in place over her eyes. Very little air seeped in, and Shabanu tried to steady her breathing to a low, shallow rhythm. In the damp monsoon heat, the musty cloth was almost suffocating, but she thought that freedom had never smelled so sweet.

Shabanu had learned to walk so silently on the rooftop it

was a habit. Even she could not hear her footfalls as she crept down the stairs—only the occasional swish of the fabric of her burqa was audible in the narrow back staircase. She paused in the shadow of the doorway and listened for sounds from the courtyard. Samiya's sweet, high voice sang out from the laundry, and Shabanu crossed to the gate, fit the key into the lock, and turned it.

As she pulled the heavy gate toward her, its hinges screeched like a hawk flying low over the Cholistan Desert in search of prey, nearly stopping her heart. Instead of waiting to see whether Samiya would come running from the laundry, she slipped through the gate and relocked it, twisting the key until she heard the bolt slide home, then ran down the alley, her heart pounding.

She slowed to a fast walk as she rounded the corner at the busy thoroughfare that led into the bazaar. It was choked with handcarts loaded down with bolts of cloth being pulled by human beasts of burden, motor scooters spewing blue smoke from their exhaust pipes, donkey carts piled high with copper pots, shoppers making their way to the produce alley.

Shabanu wandered among the spice merchants, squeezing past great pyramids of amber powdered cumin and red ground chilies and green mounds of cardamom pods, breathing in the spice scents and listening to the bartering of shoppers and the profane banter of the shopkeepers. She watched ragged boys dart in and out among the stalls of the fruit vendors, stealing hard green amrud and shining red pomegranates.

She was intoxicated by the noise and dust and activity of the bazaar, more aware than she had been in ten years of the breath passing in and out through her nose and mouth, the steady beating of her heart, and the rushing of blood through her veins. It was almost as if she had been barely alive all that time, as if her body had put itself into a semiconscious state of hibernation from which she was just now awakening.

She was careful to watch the time, and even so, barely made it home before Samiya came in from the market. She was asleep long before Selma returned from the banquet at Mahsood's house at Number 5 Anwar Road.

In the middle of the night Shabanu slipped back down the stairway to the gate and oiled the hinges so that the next day when she let herself out again it would sigh softly, just as she sighed going back to sleep.

2

Jameel and Mumtaz sat on the edge of the marble swimming pool dangling their feet in the tepid water. It was mid-monsoon, and wet heat pressed down on the city of Lahore like the heel of a giant hand. Jameel glanced over his shoulder.

"I'm watching, Jameel!" said his mother from the shade of the patio where she sipped tea with Auntie Leyla and Auntie Selma, who'd come to visit for the day. "You still have twenty minutes to wait. I don't want your grandfather to have to pull your waterlogged body from the bottom of the pool!"

Jameel closed his eyes and exhaled through his teeth. Mumtaz nudged him with her elbow.

"It's an old wives' tale, Muti," Jameel said under his breath. "You can't drown because you just ate aloo paratha."

"Five aloo paratha, maybe . . ." said Muti, smirking.

"She's never so protective in San Francisco." Jameel took a long, slow breath. "I'm fifteen years old!" They were silent for a moment. "How do you stand it?" he asked, keeping his voice low. "Your whole life happens under their noses! Don't they suffocate you?"

"Baba and Uncle Omar are okay," said Muti, absently flicking water with her toes. "Leyla would just as soon see me drown." Jameel slid his eyes over toward her. Muti knew that kind of talk made her cousin uncomfortable. Jameel visited every summer, and he liked things to run smoothly, with everyone getting along—especially with only a few days before the end of vacation.

But the fact was things seldom ran smoothly for Muti. Her mother and father had died when she was five, and most of the time since she'd lived with a woman who hated her. Leyla had also hated Muti's mother, and took every opportunity to let Muti know she was not her social equal, and that having her live with them was a terrible burden on everyone. Treating Muti as a servant whenever Baba wasn't looking was a part of Leyla's cleverly devised brand of torture, which Muti called "death by a thousand pinpricks."

"Where is everyone?" Baba's voice boomed across the gardens, which were heavy with the scent of tuberoses and jasmine. Jameel imagined that the ripples in the fountain and swimming pool came from the depth of his grandfather's voice. "I have a surprise for you! You'll never guess what's just arrived!"

Omar and Leyla's son, Jaffar, who was ten, bolted from

the shade of the banyan tree on the other side of the pool, where he'd been playing in a lawn chair with an electronic toy that bleeped wildly as he pushed the buttons. "What, Baba? What is it?" Jaffar shouted. Jameel and Muti unfolded their bodies from the pool's rim and turned toward Mahsood Jameel Amirzai, the patriarch of the family, after whom Jameel was named. The old man stood with his massive hands on his hips, his pale blue shalwar kameez hanging limply over his rotund belly, a white turban piled loosely around the crown of his head, and his beard a white tangle of curls on his chest.

He'd come from the garage, where a large motor roared to life. Jameel thought of the summer his grandfather had imported a red-and-silver BMW motorcycle from Germany, complete with a protective suit of leather—chaps, boots, and vest. The noise alone had scandalized the staid Gulberg area of Lahore almost beyond forgiveness. Grandmother didn't speak to her husband for a good part of the summer. Finally Baba had taken a nasty spill when he was showing off for his friends in the driveway, smacking his head on the pavement, and wounding his dignity more than his skull. Only then had he agreed to ride the machine exclusively in the countryside, where villagers heard him coming and dove into the thorn bushes beside the road to avoid being run down. Jameel wondered what machine had captured Baba's fancy this time.

But Baba would not let them into the garage. "It's a surprise!" he said, and everyone looked around at everyone else, eyebrows raised, which pleased the old man very much.

Within the hour Baba gathered a party together on the bank of the canal, outside the garden gate. He sent Leyla to organize tea and cake, and he called Uncle Omar to come home from his office downtown. Jameel's mother went back up to the house with Leyla, and Muti held Selma's arm as they walked to the canal's edge.

When Omar arrived at the spot beside the canal, Baba waited for Nargis and Leyla to return before pulling a tarpaulin from the back of a battered pickup truck to reveal a shining silver Jet Ski. His driver, Khoda Baksh, supervised five servants as they unloaded the machine and slid it into the slimy green water where the canal curved to run beside Anwar Road. Baba waded in and climbed aboard, revving the engine and nearly toppling off as the Jet Ski leaped to life.

Omar leaned back on his elbows, stretched his legs out before him in the grass, and laughed. Jameel's mother and Auntie Selma smiled affectionately, and Leyla put her hands over her mouth in horror.

"I'm glad your mother isn't alive to see this," Leyla hissed under her breath. Grandmother had died the year before. Omar looked at his wife and sighed.

"Mother always tolerated more than she let on," he said. "He always expected her to disapprove—and she never let him down." Since his mother's death Leyla had taken on the role of household critic. Omar shifted his attention back to the canal.

Jameel and Muti and Jaffar all clapped as Baba got the machine under control and shot down the canal with his beard flying and the end of his turban flapping over his shoulder and a bright arc of spray jetting out behind. Two turbaned malis stood from their work around the rose beds beside the canal and stared in wonder after Baba, their lungis loose around their hips, their hands holding sickles dangling by their sides.

Jaffar, Muti, and Jameel all begged for rides, and Baba took the boys first, one at a time. When he returned for Muti, Leyla marched down to the edge of the canal.

"You mustn't, Baba," she said, her eyes flashing. "All of Gulberg is laughing at you."

"Let them laugh!" Baba said loudly. "It'll add a little fun to their day!"

Leyla was stricken and unable to speak for a moment. "But . . . but . . . for Mumtaz this behavior is unseemly! You know what people will think! How will we find a suitable match for her if she behaves this way?" Leyla's voice had grown shrill. The spell of Baba's amazing machine was suspended for a moment.

"Oh, let them think!" Baba boomed, brushing aside Leyla's protests—just as he'd brushed aside his wife's objections. "Come on, Mumtaz," he said, beckoning Muti into the water. "We only live once, eh?" Muti pulled her shalwar up around her knees and waded in, the bottom mud squishing between her toes. She climbed onto the seat behind Baba. But she knew that Leyla would make her pay later, when she was out of Baba's sight.

* * *

That evening Number 5 Anwar Road overflowed with members of the Amirzai extended family. They gathered first in the large reception hall to honor Jameel and his parents amid flowers and pitchers of pomegranate juice, and whiskey, too, although Baba kept it in a teapot, and offered it quietly to the gentlemen, all of whom considered themselves good and devout Muslims.

"More cold tea?" he asked, and the men chuckled and said yes, holding out their teacups for more whiskey.

Jameel and his parents were leaving in two days to return to San Francisco, where Jameel was born and had lived his entire life. They'd arrived in Lahore the week after school ended, the third week in June, after two or three days in Karachi to visit Jameel's paternal grandparents. And now it was August, and school would begin soon.

Jameel couldn't imagine where the summer had gone. This year he'd come to Lahore reluctantly for the first time in his life. He'd met a girl in California, just before the end of the school term—a beautiful blond girl named Chloe. He couldn't wait to tell Muti about Chloe, but this summer it seemed his parents or Uncle Omar or Auntie Leyla—someone—was always around. It was as if he and Muti needed a chaperone.

Muti and Jameel had been best friends since they were toddlers. Technically, they were first cousins once removed. They were a month apart in age, and they shared secrets and jokes and dreams. As children they had made up games, instantly falling into each other's imaginings. There were dragons in trees and monsters in bushes, villains and bandits who needed routing around every corner. Evenings they'd sneaked down the back stairs to watch the adults at lavish dinners, and to listen in as Baba settled tribal disputes in his grand reception hall. They'd exchanged letters in the long fall, winter, and spring, devising plans for the summer. But this year it seemed one of the adults was always nearby and they'd had few private conversations.

When everyone moved into the dining room for the banquet, Baba upset Leyla's seating arrangement, insisting that men and women sit together at the two long tables, and the younger relatives—boys and girls together—at the smaller round tables around the edge of the room. Leyla tried to redirect ladies to one table, gents to the other in a more traditional seating arrangement, but Baba easily overpowered her with his booming voice.

Once the confusion ended and everyone was seated, a dozen bearers in white uniforms and fanned turbans brought out platter after platter: roast meat in spiced gravy, vegetables in delicately flavored sauces, biryani made with scented rice and pieces of meat, steaming piles of roti, kebabs of lamb and chicken, deep dishes of channa and lentils and pickles and dahi with cucumbers to cool the heat of the spices.

Members of Baba's family who seldom appeared at Number 5 Anwar Road were there: his brother Nazir, who lived alone and out of favor in a suburb on the road that went toward the border crossing at Wagga; their sister, Selma, who lived alone in the family's old haveli in the ancient walled city of Lahore; and cousins, aunts, and uncles whom Jameel and Muti greeted politely before joining the younger people at their own tables.

The dining room, which had a white marble floor, echoed with the sounds of laughter and talk, glasses clinking, and the ping of silverware on china plates. An enormous crystal chandelier hung overhead, its arms branching out the length of the two large tables, which seated twelve people each. Jameel and Muti and Jaffar sat at one of the smaller tables with four cousins, who ranged in age from eight to eighteen.

When they had eaten, the bearers began to clear the plates while others brought out platters of fruit and sweets—silver-covered burfi, bhoondi ladoo and bowls of coconut kheer, halwa and rasmali, pretzel-shaped jalabis—and the children's faces rekindled with smiles as each new tray arrived. Leyla rose from her place at one of the large tables and made her way around to where Muti sat, and stood facing her, hands on hips.

"Get up and help clear, Mumtaz," Leyla said. Out of the corner of her eye Muti saw Jameel look at her in surprise. "You're supposed to earn your keep." Muti glanced over toward the big table. "Omar and your grandfather have been into their cold tea," Leyla continued. "They aren't going to rescue you. Get up!" Muti got to her feet obediently, collected the remaining plates on their table, and carried them toward the kitchen. She didn't want Leyla to make more of a scene and embarrass everyone.

As she passed the end of the large table, Muti smiled at Auntie Selma. Her father's sister frowned, and did not smile back. Selma shifted her eyes toward Leyla, watching her until she resumed her seat at the large table.

When Muti was helping to serve tea, Jameel caught her eye and gave her the signal they'd always used for emergency meetings: five fingers spread on the tabletop, his head beckoning slightly with a tilt over the shoulder. It meant five minutes, out in the garden.

Muti waited until Leyla was occupied with giving more orders to the bearers, and slipped out the French doors that led to the swimming pool and the gardens beyond. She followed the path beside the pool, through the rose garden, and down to a small garden with a little pond that held Baba's silver-and-orange koi, with a wooden garden swing beside it, where Jameel sat waiting.

"What took you so long?" It was Jameel's turn to smirk. Muti sighed and sank down beside him on the swing.

"Leyla's always watching to take advantage of me. It'll be almost a relief after you've gone, when she'll simply ignore me again!" Muti said.

"Did you do something to make her angry?" he asked. Muti sighed but said nothing. Jameel had never seemed to notice before that Leyla spoke sharply to Muti, that she ordered her to do things only the servants were expected to do, and that she acted under the radar of Omar and Baba. When Muti was little, Leyla and her mother, Amina, tried to make Shabanu mend the clothing and look after the children and clean their shoes, and even Muti's father didn't seem to notice.

"We don't have much time and I want to tell you something," Jameel said, clearing his throat and turning to look at Muti. "I've met a girl I like very much. Her name is Chloe, and she's beautiful and kind. And my parents would freak out if they knew." He smiled at Muti, whose jaw had dropped.

"Where did you meet?" she asked. "Does she go to your school? Why didn't you tell me?"

"I tried! This is the first time I've had a chance," said Jameel. "We met skateboarding. She's the best skater in the park. She's amazing. She does flips and twists and ollies and . . ." Jameel remembered Muti knew nothing about skateboarding. "She goes to a different school—a public school—and my parents know nothing about her. We talked one day, and then we just started to meet at the park, after school and weekends. I almost didn't even want to come here this summer!"

Muti's eyes widened and her breath caught. "How can you say that? I thought you loved coming here. You always say it's the best part of the year!"

"It is!" Jameel said quickly. "It was just—you know. I didn't want to leave . . ."

Muti also had been looking for an opportunity to tell Jameel about Jag, the handsome tennis coach she'd met at the Lahore Club—and the most unsuitable person for her to have a crush on. But she didn't want it to seem as if she was trying to match Jameel's story. And Jameel was right. This summer they never had the time or privacy to talk.

Voices wafted through the trellis then, as if someone had

opened the French doors leading from the dining room into the rose garden. Jameel and Muti stood. They looked at each other, both struck by the same thought. They almost felt guilty.

"Mumtaz! Jameel! Where are you?" It was Leyla, and her voice moved toward them. "What do you mean by slipping away when we have guests?"

"Over here, Auntie," said Jameel, resting his hands lightly on the gate to the rose garden and leaning forward so Leyla could see him. "We were looking at Grandfather's koi—"

"In the dark? You've had all summer to look at them!" Leyla's voice rose, now that she was out of earshot of the dining room. Jameel didn't know what to say. Muti looked down at her hands and said nothing. "Come back now and say goodbye to everyone. They'll think you two have been brought up without manners."

Muti and Jameel came into the marble front foyer just as Auntie Selma drew her white lawn dupatta up over her hair. Selma had worn widow's white for more than twenty years.

"There you are, Mumtaz!" Selma said, embracing Muti and kissing her forehead. "You must come to see me."

"When can I come, Auntie?" Muti asked quickly, before Selma had a chance to get away.

"I'll call you this week," Selma said, and her eyes lingered on Muti's face.

"Yes, Auntie," said Muti. "I'll look forward to your call. I really do want to visit you." Selma laid her palm against Muti's cheek and smiled, then left as her driver pulled her old-fashioned sedan up to the door.

Every time Selma saw Muti at a family wedding or some other event, Selma looked the girl over and kissed her forehead, and asked her questions about school, her friends, and anything else going on in Muti's life. On each occasion Selma said, "You must come to see me. You and I are destined to spend some time together when the occasion is right."

But Selma never fixed a date for Muti to visit the haveli, and Muti wondered what would cause the time to be right and why her mysterious aunt felt destined to be with her. She thought of going there on her own, hiring a motor rickshaw to take her into the old walled city, near the Shahi Qila. Muti had not visited the haveli since she was a child, but she still knew how to get there.

3

Shabanu adjusted the folds of the burqa around her, lifting the hem away from her feet, and walked quickly. She had been drawn irresistibly into the smells and sounds and activity of the bazaar, just as she had been the day before. She was bolder today, venturing into conversations with merchants—a simple query as to the cost of bangles here, and there a comment to an apothecary who ground gemstones into powder for kohl to shadow the eyes.

She made her way to Munir Bookseller and told the clerk behind the counter she wanted elementary readers.

"How many?" he asked.

"Twelve," she said, and he took her to a shelf of booklets that contained rough drawings of foods with their names written under each: chawal, roti, atta; and animals: gaay, bukri, pakshi; and numbers: eek, do, teen. There was a section on telling time. And toward the back were simple sentences. Shabanu paid the bookseller and went off to find a clock to teach the desert women of Cholistan how to tell time.

Delighted with everything from the sound of her own voice speaking to strangers to the shadow of her form that followed her on the dusty pavement, she had lost track of the hour. It was nearly noon, and Selma would be coming to have lunch with her in the pavilion to tell about the banquet at Number 5 Anwar Road. Most important would be the news she brought of Mumtaz. It was Shabanu's only contact with her daughter—if one could consider observation at second hand the same thing as contact.

It was an oddity of Selma's that she would not come to the roof of the haveli at night, or at any time before noon. In the deadening heat of pre-monsoon summers, Selma and her husband, Daoud, who had been a judge in the Lahore High Court, used to sleep on the roof to catch whatever air moved high above the other buildings surrounding the haveli. One night about twenty-five years before, the brother of a murderer whom Daoud had sentenced to life in prison had taken his revenge by creeping up to the roof and burying a dagger in the heart of the judge as he slept beside his wife. Selma had slept so soundly through the heat of the night that she never knew her husband lay dead beside her until she awoke in the morning and found him in a sticky pool of his own blood. The servants believed the judge's ghost prowled the rooftop every night, and so the doors to both stairways were kept locked. Shabanu was safe in the spacious rooftop courtyard and pavilion because everyone believed the judge's ghost would haunt the place every night for eternity.

Selma had regarded her husband as the twin of her own soul and could not bear to face his apparition on the roof because she could not admit to her suspicion that she might have saved him had she slept less soundly. Shabanu found comfort in the nocturnal prowlings of Daoud's ghost, for he was her protector. She smiled when she stumbled over a potted palm that the judge's ghost moved into her path to trip her as she walked the perimeter of the roof after sunset. When she heard him humming late in the night sometimes, she took out her flute and accompanied him. When it came to ghosts, it was the djinn in Gulberg that Shabanu feared, because her daughter lived among them and Shabanu wanted desperately for her to be safe.

When Shabanu got to the weathered gray wooden doors of the outer courtyard of the haveli, she hurried past and ducked around the corner and into the alley that ran behind the old house. She picked her way over mango pits and onion peelings and shreds of plastic bags that had been tossed over the back walls of the houses at the beginning of the lane. The way was dim, shaded by the towering walls of the haveli and the houses on either side. Gray drain water sloshed up over the narrow ditches that ran along both sides of the alley.

A young man and an older woman also hurried along the lane, on their way home to their midday meal, but neither of them paid attention to her. She strode quickly to the blue-painted heavy steel gate at the back of the haveli and pulled the rusty iron key from the bundle of keys tied in a handkerchief around her wrist to keep them from jangling, and fit it into the heavy lock in the gate.

Once back inside, Shabanu shut the gate quietly behind her and relocked it, then turned to slip up the back stairway to the rooftop. Standing in her way were Selma and Samiya, their hands on their hips, their lips pursed, so that despite the differences in their age and size they almost looked alike in their widows' white saris and angry scowls.

"What are you thinking, Shabanu?" asked Selma in her sternest voice. "We have gone to such lengths to hide and protect you, even from your own family—and you slip in and out like a thief!" She made a clicking sound with her tongue, eloquent in its disapproval.

Shabanu reached out and touched the arm of her sister-in-law, who had suffered so much, had saved her life—still saved her life every day. Shabanu left her hand on Selma's arm and looked into her eyes. After a moment she pulled the burqa off and smoothed back her hair.

"I am thinking that I am not yet thirty years old, and I have been buried on the rooftop for one third of my life," she said, her voice level and reasonable. Samiya stepped forward then and took the burqa from Shabanu's hands and draped it over her arm.

"Have you forgotten Nazir?" asked Samiya. "How do you know he doesn't have spies around the city? He may look old and defeated, but how can we be sure he has given up?" Her voice shook with fear more than anger.

"I can't spend my entire life locked away," Shabanu replied. "I feel like one of those plants that's been neglected in the back of the courtyard, the ones that turn white for lack of sun and water just before their leaves begin to drop, just before they die!"

Selma and Samiya looked at each other. Shabanu was first to break the silence.

"I'm sorry," she said. "But I felt finally as if I could no longer breathe, buried alive up there."

Selma held up her hand. "You think I don't understand? You don't give me much credit. But we have something important to discuss. We can talk later about your annee-jannee nonsense—your coming and going as you please. Come." She reached for the door to the back stairway. "Samiya has made lunch and will join us upstairs."

Selma moved slowly up the stairs, one leg and then the other on each step, her arthritis flaring to bright pain every morning and through midday. Samiya disappeared into the kitchen to fix their tray. When Shabanu and Selma got to the top step, Selma went into the pavilion to get out of the hot sun. She drew the end of her embroidered white lawn sari around her shoulders and sat heavily on the wood-and-string charpoi. Selma patted the cushion beside her, inviting Shabanu to sit.

"The evening was very festive," said Selma. "Mumtaz and Jameel are lovely, and they're such good friends. You would be so proud of your daughter."

Shabanu's heart quickened at the thought of Mumtaz, whose photograph sat on the table in her room. But she also heard in Selma's voice a note of something less pleasant about to come.

Samiya brought the tray with plates of cold chicken, roti, dahi, stewed spiced lentils, and milky sweet tea. Selma and Shabanu were quiet while Samiya laid the table, then sat down with them.

"Mahsood was in rare form—as usual!" Selma smiled only slightly, and told Shabanu about the Jet Ski. "And as usual, Leyla behaved despicably." Selma recounted how Leyla had humiliated Mumtaz in front of her cousins.

"It never ends," Shabanu said when Selma had finished. She remembered that when she'd first come to the farm at Okurabad from Cholistan as Rahim's wife, she was terrified of the other women in his household. One morning someone had caught a rabid bat in a net and hid it in Shabanu's clothes cupboard. When she opened the door, the bat flew out and screeched around the room until Shabanu caught it with a broom and beat it to death on the floor. All the while she heard the stifled laughter of the women through the window that looked out onto the arbor-covered terrace at the side of the house.

Later, when Rahim learned of the bat, he was angry and demanded to know who had done such a thing. A small, thin boy, the son of a man who worked in the cattle pens, was produced as the culprit. Shabanu was certain that the women had put him up to the prank.

In the seven years of Shabanu's marriage to Rahim, his family—with the exception of Omar, Baba, and Selma—never let her forget that she was the daughter of camel herders. The women played cruel tricks on her and treated her like a servant. Rahim dismissed Shabanu's complaints and said he was too busy dealing with more important issues.

Rahim had loved Shabanu the best of all his four wives, and they never forgave her. Rahim would not tolerate dissension in the house, and so Shabanu and Mumtaz had to sleep with their eyes open and their ears tuned for trouble.

Shabanu and Mumtaz visited Lahore for the first time when Mumtaz was five. They stayed with Selma in the haveli in the Old City, which was the family's ancestral home. When Pakistan became independent from India and British colonial rule in 1947, Baba and Nazir had moved with their mother to the house in Gulberg because they wanted a more modern house than the haveli, with its unlit rooms and unplumbed baths and creaking stairs. But Rahim and Selma loved the Old City. Shabanu and Mumtaz felt safe there with Selma, untroubled by Rahim's other wives, who lived in fancier houses in the Cantonment and Gulberg. The haveli became Shabanu and Mumtaz's home.

"There is more," Selma said. "I overheard Amina and Tahira saying that Leyla has been making inquiries about a marriage for Mumtaz with a boy from the farm."

"But Omar and Mahsood would never let that happen!" said Shabanu.

"No, not together. But if something were to happen to Mahsood, I'm not sure that Leyla couldn't manipulate Omar," Selma said. "She has grown to be an indomitable force in that way."

"But Omar would never allow anything to keep Mumtaz from finishing her education!" Shabanu said. Like Rahim, Omar was a man of honor. He had known how much she wanted an education for Mumtaz, and he would see that Mumtaz finished school.

"In any case," said Selma, "we should be prepared if Omar gives in to Leyla. I think perhaps it's time you and your daughter had a reunion. She's already older than you were when you married Rahim. She's old enough to understand what happened, and old enough to keep your secret. And she still needs you—perhaps now more than ever."

Shabanu took a deep breath. It was difficult to think of Mumtaz as a young woman—impossible to think of her married to an uneducated boy in a dusty village. She had to remind herself that her daughter was no longer the five-year-old child she'd last held in her arms ten years before. Shabanu still thought of the sweet smell of milk on Mumtaz's breath, the soft curves of her small elbows and knees, the way her eyelashes fell to her cheeks as she fought sleep at nap time.

"I agree," said Shabanu. "Mumtaz and I should become reacquainted—as soon as possible. What shall we do about Nazir?"

"He was there last night," said Selma. "He's different, Shabanu—he's like a toothless old tiger now. He's failed at every scheme he's plotted. He's been abandoned by his family, and he looks pathetic. His only interest is his airplane, and I don't think he's flown it in ages. His clothes aren't clean, he needs shaving, and heaven knows how long since he's had a haircut. He barely spoke to anyone last evening, and I saw no one speak to him."

Shabanu thought of the day she and Omar went with Rahim to confront Nazir over the theft of some of Rahim's land. Nazir's men had cut down the trees and fenced off several dozen hectares, and Nazir's cattle grazed there. Rahim was just stepping from the car when bullets began to fly. Several slammed into Rahim and knocked him to the ground, and Omar, whom Shabanu loved more than she could now remember, exposed himself to the bullets, leaping from the car and pulling Rahim back inside, blood seeping through his uncle's clothing. Shabanu didn't see the shooter, but her mind's eye captured Nazir's fleshy face bunched in a squint as he took aim down the barrel of his gun and killed his brother. She heard Nazir's heavy breathing, felt it on her face as he demanded that she marry him.

After Rahim's death, Nazir had kidnapped her and Zabo, his own daughter and Shabanu's only friend, and held them prisoner in a damp, dark room in the depth of the house on his farm near Rahim's at Okurabad. She watched him pluck a cockroach from the floor, heard its shell shatter as he pinched it between his fingers to show that he held the same power over her, and felt its insides splatter on her face and clothing.

And when they escaped, Shabanu felt Zabo's arms around her waist as they fled from Nazir's farm into the desert by camel—until she heard the impact of a bullet piercing

Zabo's back, and her friend slumped against her shoulder. She stopped only when they were safely inside the gate of the fort at Derawar. She saw Zabo's eyes close in her pale face and felt her last shuddering breath. So much death, so much fear, so much loss caused by Nazir and the penchant that men had for taking revenge.

"You must never trust a tiger, even a miserable, toothless old tiger," said Shabanu.

Shabanu told Selma and Samiya then how she had broken the spell Nazir had cast over her by sending the pigeon to her family with the message that she was alive, and by leaving the haveli, showing the fates that fear no longer held her in its grip.

Selma took Shabanu's hands in both of hers. "You're right," Selma said. "You cannot live here forever. You still have a whole life before you!"

Shabanu held Selma's gaze, but she did not answer. One more memory crowded into her mind's eye: she saw Omar kneeling beside Zabo's grave inside the walls of Derawar Fort, thinking it was Shabanu's. He threw back his head and howled like a jackal, and a chill skipped down between her shoulder blades. It was a long time ago, she reminded herself.

* * *

Shabanu did not go out into the bazaar again. She thought of everything she wanted to say to Mumtaz, and she waited for the bird from Okurabad. Both times in the bazaar she'd imagined seeing Mumtaz in the distance, recognizing her daughter under her burqa out of sheer love.

She kept busy by arranging photographs of her mother and father for Mumtaz to see, photos of her wedding, with Rahim looking young and handsome, although he was forty years older than Shabanu. She had waited for ten years, and these last days or hours before Mumtaz's visit seemed to go on forever. Shabanu was impatient, because waiting felt like the old life, and she did not want to go back to her old self.

On the fourth day after she'd released Barra into the sky, another pigeon appeared at the wire enclosure, a plump brown bird with a green head and splatters of black and gold on her breast—a pigeon as old as Barra. The bird circled the roof—almost as if she wasn't sure she remembered the place where Rahim had called her home—until Shabanu noticed her. When Shabanu opened the wire enclosure, she flew in as if she'd only been gone for an afternoon's flight, instead of having been almost a lifetime away from home.

With trembling fingers Shabanu unlatched the compartment attached to the bird's leg. Inside was a small piece of featherweight blue rice parchment even lighter than the one she had sent Ibne.

The Sun has risen! In its vast dazzle
Every lamp is drowned.

In answer to Shabanu's note Ibne had quoted another timeless, graceful poem by Rumi. Ibne had been just as cautious, letting her know that he and her family rejoiced in the knowledge she was alive, but not fixing a date when they might see each other again.

4

Can you give me a lift to Fariel's?" Muti asked as Omar stood up from the breakfast table and wiped his lips with a linen napkin. It was the week after Jameel and his parents had left for America, a monsoon morning that smelled lush and damp.

"Does her mother know you're coming?" Leyla asked without looking up from her newspaper. "You shouldn't be pestering them. Fariel will be having her school clothes made this week." Leyla tapped her bright crimson fingernails on the table.

"Five minutes," said Omar, setting his napkin beside his plate.

"Yah," Muti said, swallowing the rest of her sweet lime juice in one gulp. "Fariel and I're going with Shaheen to the bazaar to look for fabric. Their darzi is making school clothes for both of us."

"Really, Mumtaz," Leyla said, "why do you say 'yah'? You do it just to annoy me!"

"Sorry," said Muti, lowering her eyes. But she was not in the least sorry. A long time ago Muti had heard Leyla mutter under her breath, "She's a low-born Gypsy just like her mother." Remembering always made Muti want to behave like a Gypsy. And sometimes that compulsion cost her dearly.

"Sorry, what?" Leyla demanded, and Muti looked straight at her.

"Sorry, Auntie," she said, her eyes holding Leyla's until Leyla was forced to look away.

Leyla was not her auntie at all but a half sister—they were both Rahim's daughters. Leyla insisted, however, that if Muti was to live with her and Omar, she must call her Auntie. And Omar was not Muti's uncle but her cousin. Baba was not her grandfather but her uncle. Muti had learned at a tender age that very little in her world was what it appeared. She went along with Leyla's version of family relations to keep peace—if this uneasy tiptoeing around could be called peace. Muti had grown accustomed to the shifting ground that was her family.

* * *

After Muti's mother and father died, she'd been sent to live with her mother's family in the Cholistan Desert. Although her grandparents and Auntie Sharma were kind to her, Muti missed her mother terribly. She never stopped watching the horizon for her mother's return, and her stomach ached constantly.

One day Muti thought her prayers had been answered. Shortly after sunrise on a spring day, a tall horseman appeared like an apparition from behind a sand dune. He rode his fine black stallion deliberately toward where Muti sat helping her grandmother roast roti on a flat black pan over a small hot fire.

The rider was Omar, and when she saw him she jumped up and ran to him. She threw her arms around his neck when he got down from his horse and knelt to say hello. "Have you come to take me to my mother?" she asked. She thought of the happy days at the haveli when Omar had been her mother's friend and was part of their lives.

Her grandmother hushed her and sent her to fetch her grandfather, who was at the well, hauling water for the camels. Omar looked very much like his Uncle Rahim, and the old woman easily guessed who he was.

They all shook hands several times, and Mumtaz's grandfather held on to Omar's hand after the introduction was over. Shabanu's parents had loved their son-in-law. They invited Omar to sit with them on a dhurrie beside the cooking fire. Muti and her grandmother poured tea and offered Omar freshly roasted roti, which he ate while he explained why he'd come.

"Shabanu's fondest wish was that Mumtaz should go to school," Omar said. Grandfather said nothing, and Grandmother looked down at her hands. "I've come to bring her back to Lahore to live with my family and to attend St. Agnes Academy." More silence followed.

"Mumtaz is all that we have left of our Shabanu," Grandfather said finally. "We would not like to let her go." At that, Grandmother raised her eyes.

"We would miss her terribly," she said. "But she has been here for several months and still she has not adjusted well. Perhaps she would do better in the city where she remembers living with her mother and father." And so it had been decided, and Muti had lived with Baba and Omar, Leyla, and their son, Jaffar, ever since.

* * *

"May I please leave the table?" Muti asked, standing abruptly.

"I want you back by teatime," Leyla said. "Your cousins are coming, and I want you to help." Muti set her mouth. What Leyla meant was they were having their weekly tea party, and Muti would serve them all cakes and tea, and then she would look after her little cousins and nieces and nephews to keep them out of their mothers' hair so the women might gossip in peace.

Babysitting and serving tea were not very high on the scale of pinpricks. The worst pinprick underlay all that Leyla said and did. Muti knew that Leyla would evict her from the house with the least provocation. But like a moth drawn to flame, Muti could not keep herself from provoking Leyla.

Muti also knew Baba and Omar wouldn't let anything happen to her. And so Muti and Leyla struggled in a perverse tug-of-war.

"Yes, Auntie," Muti said, her eyes still lowered. "Um—bye!" She turned from the table abruptly and ran out through the arch into the front hallway, her bare feet slapping on the cool marble floor.

"Stop running!" Leyla shouted after Muti. "And since when do we come to the table without shoes?" Muti pretended she hadn't heard and took the steps two at a time.

She stopped outside the doorway to Baba's bedroom/sitting room to say good morning. Muti couldn't love Baba more if he really were her grandfather. Through the partly open door she heard the restless movement of his legs under the bed linens. She stepped closer and tapped softly on the doorframe.

"Baba?" she whispered. There was no answer. She knocked again and peered around the doorframe in time to see a flash of what looked like a small ball of extraordinarily bright firelight just over Baba's form in the bed. Her heart leaped, but the flash disappeared so quickly she thought perhaps she hadn't seen it at all. Normally Muti was not one to doubt herself. But this time the spacious room lay dim, and she wondered whether her eyes hadn't deceived her.

She tiptoed into the room. She wondered if the flash had come from outside. She pulled back the heavy green velvet drape and looked down over the garden. Could it have been a reflection of the sunlight from something on the ground—the mirror of a car? Or from something overhead—a small, low-flying airplane? She let the drape fall back over the window and turned around. Baba seemed quieter now, and she decided to let him sleep. Her dear Baba had seemed to slow down at times these last few weeks. Sometimes he seemed to have no energy, and other times he was his old self. She must keep a closer eye on him, she thought as she tiptoed out and into the hallway that led to her own room.

Muti sat on the bed and slipped her favorite worn sandals onto her feet. She stuffed a pair of white churidar pajama, the closer-fitting drawstring trousers she wore for tennis, into her duffel with a folded, fresh white tunic, a towel, and her tennis shoes and racket.

Tugging at the back of her mind was another peculiar event of a few days earlier—the day after Jameel left. That early morning she awoke suddenly, as if something had disturbed her sleep. She sat up and squinted at the luminous hands of the clock on the bedside table. They pointed to five-thirty. She swung her bare feet over the side of the bed and got up. She didn't bother turning on the light because she knew the bathroom was a clear shot across the bare floor. Muti had taken to cleaning her bedroom every day so that Leyla would not have that to complain about. Just a few feet from her bed she tripped over something soft. Each step took her deeper into what seemed to be a sea of clothing.

She flipped the switch to the overhead light when she reached the wall next to the bathroom door, and was amazed to see that someone had emptied every hanger and shelf of her closet onto the floor. Towels were spread around the bathroom as if someone had used each one and discarded it. When she had gone to bed both rooms were as neat and tidy as if the ayah had just been there, followed by the sweeper with his dust cloths and whisk broom. Muti crossed to her closet and threw open the doors. The hangers were empty and knocked askew, where they had been evenly spaced on the bar before she'd gone to bed; the shelves were empty. She knew very well that she had taken to folding every shawl and dupatta neatly and stacking them with mathematical precision on top of every other shawl and dupatta.

It was absurd to think someone had crept into her room in the middle of the night and turned it upside down. Muti would never have slept through it. She had spent the rest of the early morning hours before breakfast returning everything to its proper place. The entire time she thought about how this chaos might have fallen on her room. While she did not suffer from self-doubt, neither was she one to keep a closed mind.

Muti thought of the day early in the summer when she and Jameel had asked Baba to tell them about the djinn. They were in the garage, where Baba was under the hood of the car, working on the ancient engine of his Mercedes Benz. Khoda Baksh held tools for him, and they talked softly as Baba worked.

"Baba," Muti had said, "please tell Jameel the story of Great-grandfather and the djinn. He doesn't believe me."

"I just don't believe that the house is haunted," Jameel said, "that the djinn have always lived here."

Baba came out from under the hood of the car and

straightened. He reached for a cloth and wiped his hands.

"Let's go up to the house and get some tea," Baba said. When they were seated in the old wicker chairs beside the pool, Baba told his story.

"When I was Jaffar's age," he began, "my father died. I didn't believe he was gone because I still saw him once or twice every week. Sometimes he'd come into my room and wake me up to talk. Sometimes he'd come into the house when I was the only one there. Sometimes he appeared as a very bright light that moved freely around the room."

"Couldn't anyone else see him?" asked Jameel. "How do you know it wasn't just your imagination?"

"The Quran says that God creates a djinni for each one of us. It's the djinni's job to lead us astray, to cause mischief in order that we should learn from the tricks he plays. A djinni can even cause harm—but his purpose is to improve us, sometimes even through temptation. Everyone has a djinni. Mine just happened to be in the form of the spirit of my father."

"Why was your djinni in the form of your father?" Jameel asked. "And why doesn't every house have djinn if the Quran says they're supposed to help us?"

"The maulvis say Allah created djinn as fiery beings that can fly and take the shape of animals or humans—they can really take any shape, and they can pass through solid objects like walls. I've asked the Maulvi Inayatullah why this house has them. He says the Quran doesn't explain why they appear to some people and not to others. He believes this house is hospitable to them for some reason."

"So why do you think they're at Number 5 Anwar Road?" Jameel asked.

"Since Allah created man with free will, I believe he put the djinn here to trick us into finding our own path. Perhaps it's because we're tribal leaders. Finding the right way ourselves, we believe more faithfully than we would otherwise."

Jameel was still dubious when the conversation was over. And Muti didn't know what to think.

"I'd believe anything Baba says," Muti said to Jameel later. "I just don't know what he means because I've never seen a djinni."

Now she thought perhaps she'd seen the first evidence of a djinni at Number 5 Anwar Road.

But it also was possible that Leyla was behind the disruption of Muti's room, just as she often was behind other disruptions in Muti's peace—death by a thousand pinpricks.

Muti came back downstairs and left her canvas duffel beside the front door. She hesitated in the front hall before returning to the dining room to ask Leyla to check on Baba in a little while. Leyla disapproved of tennis, and Muti didn't want the scolding to start all over again. She didn't want to be told today, of all days, that she couldn't go to the Lahore Club.

She did not even consider telling Leyla about the strange flash of light. Leyla might try to use it as proof that Muti was unbalanced, perhaps suggesting a new ploy to remove Muti from the house for good. Muti resolved to ask Baba more about the djinn and their proclivities for light.

". . . and you let her get away with anything," she heard Leyla say from the dining room. Her voice was harsh and bitter. Muti stopped outside the doors. A silence followed. "I put up with her because you have inflicted her on me. I do it for you, but you won't discipline her." Muti heard Omar sigh.

"I'll speak to her," he said quietly. "But it would help if you didn't always find fault—"

"Really, Omar," Leyla said, "if I could think of someone suitable at Okurabad I would seriously consider arranging her marriage. We can't put it off forever." Omar interrupted, but Muti didn't wait to hear what he said. She picked up her tennis things and headed out the front door, forgetting everything but her need to escape. Because her hands were full the door slammed, and she heard Leyla shout something from the dining room.

Muti hated being at the center of these overblown storms. She tried to pretend she was oblivious to them. It was not the first time Leyla had threatened to arrange a village marriage for Muti, but the thought chilled her. This was more than a pinprick—and the pinprick level was unusually high for so early in the day.

When Khoda Baksh saw Muti, he smiled broadly, saluted, and opened the trunk. Muti dropped her duffel in and saluted him back, then slipped into the white-linen-covered backseat, where she leaned forward so the cooled air from the vent blew on her face.

Leyla had tried to send her back to Cholistan half a dozen times that Muti could remember. Omar had always intervened, and the storm died down. Muti knew that Baba would never allow Leyla to send her away.

Often a strange melancholy settled over Muti after one of Leyla's storms. It wasn't only that Muti missed her mother and father, which she did. But the sadness had more to do with everyone else having a place in the family except for her. Everyone else was safe and secure. Only Baba and Omar loved her—and Jameel. But Baba was old and wouldn't be there to protect her forever. Omar had to keep the peace, and sometimes gave in to Leyla's demands rather than fighting continually. With Jameel gone, Muti felt as if she dangled from a thin filament, nothing but danger above, below, and all around her.

Omar appeared in a crisp shirt and trousers. It wasn't even eight in the morning, and Muti's dupatta hung limply over her shoulders. Undisciplined curls sprang from the bun at the back of her neck. Omar always looked as if he was in air-conditioned comfort, no matter what the temperature was.

"Mumtaz," he said, settling beside her in the backseat while Khoda Baksh put his briefcase in the trunk. Omar's forehead was wrinkled and his eyes were pleading.

"I know, I know!" Muti wailed. "It seems I'm tormenting her, when really she's tormenting me!" Omar looked at her for a moment without speaking.

"I heard her!" Muti said. "She wants to marry me off to some village boy!"

"That won't happen," Omar said, taking her hand. "She's just upset. I promised your grandparents and Auntie Sharma that we'll honor your mother's wish—that you'll finish school. And that is precisely what will happen."

Muti didn't answer. She sat back in the seat and breathed deeply. She knew how she needed Omar and Baba on her side. And she thought of the risk she took by meeting Jag. She knew she'd have to break it off with him. She didn't want to give Leyla a real excuse to send her away.

"It isn't easy for her, Muti," Omar went on. "She likes things to be . . . just *so*—you know, everything in order and smooth. It's difficult, too, because this is an old house, and it has some very queer things about it. I've grown up here—I'm used to it. But I have to keep in mind that it isn't easy for Leyla."

"What queer things?" Muti asked. She thought of telling him about the flame she'd seen hovering over Baba's form in the bed, and about the chaos in her bedroom. But Omar rushed on.

"And you always act as if you don't know any better. You go in your bare feet and wear those desi chappals instead of proper ladies' sandals, you chew on your fingernails instead of having manicures, you talk like a street urchin, you twist your hair—"

"Hah!" said Muti, her eyes flashing. "You know this has nothing to do with acting like a lady. You know I will never be one. And if I were, she would still never accept me, not even if every hair lay flat and precise on my head! Not even if my fingernails were bright red like hers, and I went to her fancy darzi and had my dupattas sewn with little rubies. Nothing I ever do will be right!" She surprised herself by choking on her last words. She turned her head to look out the window as Khoda Baksh pulled into the maddening crush of traffic at the end of the maidan. She brushed angrily at her tears with the back of her hand.

"Muti," Omar said. "You know I understand. You are wonderful just as you are, and you will always be perfect to me. You are so like your mother. That's probably the main reason this is so difficult for your Auntie Leyla."

Muti searched his face for a moment for some sign of the connection between him and her mother, but the familiar scrim of good-humored concern had slipped back into place, and she saw nothing. She sniffed loudly one last time. Omar shook his head and smiled.

She was about to remind Omar that he had promised not to take part in the charade that Leyla was her auntie. He knew that Leyla had shuffled the generations of the Amirzai family like a deck of cards because she thought it gave her more control over everyone. But Muti'd had enough for one day.

"Right!" she said, emphatically changing the subject. "Will Khoda Baksh be able to pick me up in time to be there for tea? I know she'll never forgive me if I'm not there to serve her tea."

Omar sighed. "Yes. I'm tied up all afternoon, anyway. He can drop you off and then come back to the office for me later." He looked out the window and seemed to study the neatly clipped monsoon-green grass along the roadway. Two months of rain had washed the trees clean, and their leaves sparkled in the misty morning light. "Turn your mobile on so I can reach you, and call me when you want Khoda Baksh. And, Muti, please leave your tennis things in the car when you get back. I'll hand them over to the dhobi when I get home. And please . . . please don't antagonize her." The shining old Mercedes sedan pulled into the parking place in front of the office on the Mall, where Muti suspected Omar went every day to escape his wife.

"Thanks," she said, rewarding him with a grin. "You are only the best!"

"And could you possibly refrain from saying 'yah' around the house?" He leaned back inside the car for one last plea. She bit her lips and nodded slightly, then smiled again. "See you later, Mango," he said. She wiggled her fingers at him and, remembering her baba suddenly, called him back.

"Baba was restless when I looked in on him just before we left," Muti said. "He's stayed in bed late every morning lately. Maybe you should call Leyla and have her check up on him." Omar nodded and waved at her again. She watched his broad shoulders disappear into the shadow of the doorway leading to his office.

5

Jameel slung his Dogtown skateboard under his arm and headed for the back door. Just as he laid his hand on the knob, Asma stepped out of the pantry and handed him a paper bag which he knew contained a well-balanced lunch: a cheese sandwich on whole grain bread, baby carrots, a carton of milk, and a plum. Jameel loved Asma, who had been his ayah since he was born. But he hated being treated like a child. He resisted the impulse to hand it back to her and tucked it inside his windbreaker.

"Thanks," he said, smiling in response to her loving gaze and letting himself out the back door. Jameel timed his departures for Pier 7 carefully. If his mother was awake she would insist on having Javed—Asma's husband—drive him, and she would badger him into saying when he'd be ready to be picked up. Jameel returned to the house at a different time each evening to discourage anyone from picking him up. Because of this strategy Jameel didn't hang out with any particular group at the pier, where most of the guys came and went in groups. It gave him time to practice carves and grinds on the concrete ramps.

It was an essential San Francisco day. The fog hung so heavily in the air that in another city it might have been called rain. His orange high-tops were soaked with dew from the grass before he was halfway to the garage. In the garage he let his board clatter to the pavement and pedaled through the open overhead door, pushing the button to close it as he passed, then down the alley onto Gough Street. From there it was a long slow coast down to the trolley line. If he timed the traffic lights just right he could skate the whole distance without stopping.

Jameel got to Pier 7 before eight o'clock, but he wasn't the first one there. Carving down the concrete walls along the steps was Chloe, the blond girl who lived for skateboarding and could outskate most of the guys. Her hair was a shining pale gold that moved smoothly around her head like liquid as she soared down the ramp. Jameel wanted to reach out and touch it. She was going down the longest ramp backside, goofy-footed, and he held his breath.

He approached quietly. As Chloe hit the end of the ramp her feet left the board and she did a heel flip, parting company with the deck of her board and tucking just in time to avoid slamming into the concrete. She rolled down the slope of the sidewalk so gracefully the slam almost seemed part of the ollie. She stood and brushed off her jeans, then flexed her neck from side to side gingerly before retrieving her board.

"You could have killed yourself," Jameel said quietly, and

Chloe whirled to face him. "Sorry, I didn't mean to scare you." She stood with her arms raised at her sides, as if she would bolt and run. When she saw it was Jameel her face relaxed into a friendly smile.

"Hey, Osama!" she said. He'd gotten over the nickname. All the guys at the pier called him Osama. Jameel knew they didn't think he was a terrorist. They called him Jimmy most of the time, because Jameel was too different. He ducked his head because he knew he was blushing. He looked up and was astonished by the blue of her eyes, just as he'd been the first time he saw them and every time since. Everyone had a nickname at the pier. The guys called her Blue because of her eyes. But Jameel loved the name Chloe. "What're you doing here so early?" Chloe was the only one besides Jameel who usually came early or stayed late. He tried not to hope he'd see her every time he turned the corner.

Chloe was at the pier more than any of the regular skaters. Jameel had the impression when he first met her that she lived nearby, perhaps in the streets. She wore tattered, clean jeans that hung from her hips, but that's what all the cool kids wore. Chloe said she lived in the Tenderloin, on Turk Street, in an apartment with her mother.

"I wanted to do some runs before the cops get here," he said, feeling tongue-tied. He imagined his father hearing those words and mentally winced. He hoped it didn't show. Skating was illegal at the pier, but in recent weeks the police had been leaving kids alone unless there were too many of them. It was one of the most popular places to skate in the city. Usually a good crowd showed up on Saturday, and it was only a matter of time before patrol cars cruised along the waterfront and the skateboarders scattered.

"Yeah, it's getting pretty crowded here, especially on weekends," Chloe said. "Come on!" They skated for an hour, crossing and recrossing each other's paths, their wheels rasping in a snappy rhythm until they stopped to rest.

"Did you ever notice," Chloe said, "that time seems to stop at the top of every ollie? I swear that second is four times longer than every other second." She sat down on her board next to Jameel. They both leaned against the chain-link fence that ran along the concrete. Jameel nodded his head enthusiastically.

"And usually," he said, squinting as the sunlight penetrated the foggy mist, "the very best seconds are the shortest ones of all. Like when you're eating the last bite of an ice cream cone?"

Chloe was studying the nose of her board, which had been reglassed several times. Jameel also noticed her wheels were worn down.

"That's what I mean, Jimmy," she said. "What better second is there than the one where you hang at the top of an ollie? It's like you really are defying gravity. And yet it's not short like the other best seconds. It's longer than even the worst seconds . . ."

"Longer than when you do math homework," said Jameel, pulling a face. Chloe laughed, and it sounded like the silver bell his mother rang to call Asma from the kitchen to clear the table after dinner.

Tourists walked along the waterfront, but Jameel and

Chloe pretty much had the ramps to themselves. Jameel forgot about the lunch he carried. When the sun burned the last traces of the fog off and the air grew warmer, he took off his windbreaker and the embarrassing brown bag fell to the concrete. He snatched it up and did an arching free throw in the direction of the garbage barrel over by the fence. Chloe's hand shot out and caught it before it hit the rim.

"What've you got?" she asked, peering into the bag. "I'm starving."

"Help yourself," said Jameel. She grinned and tore away the brown paper to get at the food. Jameel liked Chloe's free and easy way. She said what she thought and felt without having to stop and think about it. She was natural. To someone who felt smothered by his mother and his ayah and his aunties as Jameel did, Chloe's freedom was amazing. The complex relationships among his family members made him crave simple openness, which was just Chloe's style.

"Want some?" she asked, holding out the little plastic bag of carrots.

"I'll trade you the whole lunch for teaching me how to do a McTwist," Jameel said. A snap of wind tossed her golden hair sideways across her face, and he leaned forward to brush it out of her eyes. He stopped, startled yet again by their Pacific blue intensity. He leaned closer, and was about to kiss Chloe when he felt a strange shiver ripple across his shoulder blades.

He sat back on his heels. He felt as if a hand had grabbed him by the collar and yanked him away from Chloe's lips, as if they were dangerous.

"I've gotta go," Jameel said, standing and flipping his board, catching it in one graceful movement.

"Why?" Chloe said, shaking her head in disbelief. Her eyes had closed in anticipation of her first kiss from this handsome, mysterious guy. "What's wrong?"

"I don't know," he said. "I just had this weird feeling . . ."

Chloe bit her lower lip, trying not to smile. She didn't want him to think she was laughing at him. "Did it ever occur to you, Jimmy, that a weird feeling is a good thing when you're about to kiss someone you like?"

Jameel swallowed hard. He suddenly saw himself through his mother's warm dark eyes. Here he was kneeling on the ground fully intending to kiss a blond, blue-eyed girl in tattered blue jeans. With his father's ears he heard the trash talk about coming early to the pier to avoid the cops. He sensed their disapproval, their disappointment.

Most of the time Jameel felt stuck: stuck between San Francisco, where he was Jimmy, and Lahore, where he was Jameel, and between the now of California and the ancient way of thinking that was Pakistan. He was too Pakistani to fit entirely into America and too American to fit easily into Pakistan. Sometimes all Jameel, and other times all Jimmy. Stuck.

"I'm sorry, Chloe," he said, and turned toward the gate in the ten-foot chain-link fence that led to Embarcadero Street. Before he was halfway there he heard the wheels of Chloe's board as she pedaled it back toward the ramps.

6

Khoda Baksh pulled out into the heavy traffic after dropping Omar at his office and headed back toward Anwar Road. Muti hugged herself and took a deep breath. Her heart felt like a yo-yo—thrilled at one moment that she was about to see Jag, and plummeting the next because she knew she must resolve not to see him anymore. Sooner or later she and Fariel would be caught. But the excitement had been too, too irresistible. And, Muti thought, what had started out to be fun was turning into something much more significant—something much more dangerous and difficult to end.

The car turned into the welcoming, chaotic courtyard off Mustafa Road in the Cantonment area of Lahore, where Fariel lived with her widowed mother, her older sister Shaheen and Shaheen's husband, two married brothers and their wives, and at least, it seemed, a dozen children. The noise and dust of the traffic-clogged road were replaced by billowing mountains of bougainvillea, thick-trunked palm trees, the sparkle of a fountain in the center of the courtyard, and the piercing shrieks of the children, who ruled the gardens as fiercely as the ayah ruled inside the house.

Fariel sat on the veranda with her mother under the shade of a vine-laden pergola. Fariel's legs were drawn up in the rattan swing, and she hugged her knees. Fariel's mother held open her arms for Muti. Fariel jumped to her feet and took the duffel bag so Muti could lean down and receive her hug.

"How are things, darling?" Fariel's mother always treated Muti as a daughter, and to Muti it was like a cool drink of water to a thirsty traveler. She returned the hug with an extra squeeze. "Sit, sit," said Fariel's mother. "I'm sending you off with a thermos of tea, and it's not ready yet."

Shaheen's son, Rafiq, raced past with his cricket bat poised, and snagged the handle of a wicker basket that sat on the table. The ayah had filled it with Fariel's favorite lemon cream biscuits. Muti chased Rafiq down and pinned his elbows to his sides. She brought him back laughing and squirming, the basket unharmed in his hand.

"I never get special biscuits made for me," said Rafiq, scowling.

"Hah!" said Fariel. "You steal them before they're out of the oven!" She took the basket and selected two of the fragrant lemon biscuits, which she put on a plate and handed to Rafiq. "Now sit, and eat them like a human being." Rafiq snatched them up and stuffed them both into his mouth. He ran off laughing, crumbs flying.

"That boy was naughty from the moment of birth," said

Fariel's mother, shaking her head. "So, Mumtaz, tell me. Do you miss Jameel?" Muti felt tears sting at the back of her eyes and her throat tightened. She nodded and changed the subject. Yes, she missed her cousin, who did more to make her feel at home in the house at Number 5 Anwar Road than anyone, more even than Baba, who had to defend her all the time. Jameel was always happy to see her and loved her just as she was. He thought she was funny and smart—not a problem.

They talked about the weather: more rain in the afternoon, the radio had said, so they'd best get their tennis in while it was nice this morning. Muti and Fariel exchanged looks. A chill of guilt trickled down Muti's back like a drop of cold water. She loved these normal conversations that happened without a hint of rancor, their only aim comfort and sharing. She loved this house, where children were safe even when they were naughty.

Sometimes when Leyla seemed close to evicting Muti with one of her manipulative schemes, Muti fantasized about coming to live with Fariel's family. In reality there was not an inch of spare space in the crowded house.

Shaheen came downstairs from the suite of rooms she and her husband shared with their children, and they all stood. Muti hugged Fariel's mother again. The family's old ayah came out with a new basket packed with biscuits wrapped in a napkin, and now, too, a bundle of roasted chicken, and a battered thermos of iced tea. Fariel's mother inspected the basket to be sure they had everything they'd need, and added a bunch of grapes from a plate on the table. Then they were off with Shaheen driving the white Pajero, Muti and Fariel in the backseat.

Their first stop was the Shahnawaz Tailor Shop in the old Anarkali Bazaar. Shaheen stopped at the end of one of the cloth alleys. Muti and Fariel adjusted their chadors over their heads and stepped out into the stifling morning heat.

"I'll pick you up at nine-thirty sharp," Shaheen said. Parking near the bazaar was impossible, and Shaheen was off to run errands while Fariel and Muti were being fitted for three school uniforms apiece. They hurried down the dim alley, which was covered with ragged tarpaulins stretched from rooftop to rooftop to keep the rain and blazing sun from the shops below. They linked hands and ran, dodging handcarts filled with bolts of cloth, spools of thread, metal tins, and clay jars.

They waited on the bench in the front room of the cramped tailor shop while in the back room the darzi danced around one of their schoolmates and her sister, his mouth pursed around a bunch of pins, clucking and marking the pale blue fabric he'd draped about them with a nub of yellow chalk. An old, white-painted ceiling fan turned lazily overhead, stirring the linty dust and heat.

"Jag called this morning," Fariel whispered close to Muti's ear.

"He called you at home?" Muti asked, looking around to see if anyone could hear. Nobody was paying attention, but she lowered her voice anyway.

"Rafiq was supposed to have a tennis lesson this afternoon, and Jag had to change the time. It happened that I answered the phone. He asked if we were coming this morning, and I told him we were. He sounded relieved." Muti studied the tips of her toes.

"I told him last time," said Muti, "that I might not be able to come today. Omar is fine with our tennis. He covers for me by taking my clothes in to the laundry so Leyla won't see them. But she never misses anything. I know she suspects—she always suspects me of something."

"It's not as though there's anything wrong with playing tennis," said Fariel. "Half the girls in the school play."

"You know it's not the tennis," Muti said. "She disapproves of everything I do. And the others aren't sneaking around to meet a handsome tennis coach afterward! If they found out, Jag could lose his job, and she would send me away." Fariel cocked her head, but said nothing. Muti knew Fariel thought she was exaggerating.

Jag was nice and funny and he had the most beautiful eyes. Muti wasn't sure when their playful conversations had turned serious. Sometimes she felt as if Jag were a sea and she were lost in him. The thought of ending their friendship put a lump in her throat and made her eyes sting. She had tried to tell Jag the last time she'd seen him, but he wouldn't let her.

Muti hadn't even been able to tell Fariel how she felt—Fariel, who had known every secret of Muti's heart since she came to Lahore. Fariel still thought they were just having a good time.

After they had tried on their uniforms they threaded their

way back through the bazaar. The Pajero was stopped halfway down the lane, which was blocked by donkeys and people pulling carts into the bazaar. Fariel and Muti pushed and jostled their way through the crush of bodies and loaded carts.

They got into the back of the car, and Muti's heart began to race. It was partly excitement at the thought of seeing Jag, but it was also dread at the thought of telling him she must not meet him anymore. She thought of what Fariel had asked a few weeks before.

"Do you like Jagdish all that much?" Fariel had asked. "Or are you rebelling against your family?" Muti hadn't answered immediately. She wanted to think about it, to answer her friend honestly. She was certain now that the danger of being found out was a terrible thing, an impediment to—and not an exciting element of—her feelings for Jag. Whenever she thought of the things that stood in their way her heart felt heavy, because Jag—well, Jag was the most unsuitable person she could ever have fallen in love with. She knew nothing about love, but she was certain she had fallen in love with him.

It felt as if she'd stumbled, and before she could catch herself she realized she didn't want to. Falling in love in itself was forbidden and dangerous. But there was more. His name was Jagdish Sethi, and he was a Hindu. His father was from India, and Jag was here visiting his mother's family for the summer. Muti thought that even her grandfather would disapprove of her having a Hindu boyfriend.

Shaheen let Muti and Fariel off at the entrance to the Lahore Club. Teak fans turned overhead, stirring the fronds of the ferns in planters on the front porch. The girls made their way to the chintz-smothered ladies' changing room, which smelled of camphor from mothballs that stood in the drains, and ginger blossoms, which were bunched into vases on vanities and tables. They changed from their shalwar to churidar, and sat on white wicker chairs to tie their tennis shoes. They retied their long, white-lawn dupattas loosely, the tails hanging down between their shoulder blades.

They walked out onto the veranda and sank into more chintz-cushioned rattan furniture that had been drawn together under a green canopy. From there they could see every one of the tennis courts.

"You're so quiet," Fariel said. "Is something wrong?" Muti sighed deeply and looked into Fariel's cinnamon-colored eyes.

"I can't do this anymore," said Muti. Fariel cocked her head and Muti went on quickly before her friend could object. "I'm beginning to care too much for Jag. I think I've fallen in love." Women were coming off the courts, taking chairs at small tables and ordering nimbu pani with salt-not-sugar, and dabbing at their sweat-damp faces with small white towels.

"Oh, oh!" said Fariel, lowering her voice so no one could hear. "I was afraid this might happen. Are you telling him today?"

Muti nodded. Her unruly heart lurched around in her chest, and for the third time that day she felt tears burn in the back of her throat. "If I can summon the strength," she said. "But I have to. Today I heard Leyla telling Omar she wanted to arrange a marriage for me in Okurabad."

Fariel's eyes grew wide, but their coach had come out and was motioning them onto the court. By the time they lined up on the baseline with two other girls, Muti's resolve had begun to falter. Jag waited on the next court for three boys to take their rackets out of their bags. He studied the strings of his racket, adjusting them with his thumb. He looked up and saw Muti as their coach instructed them to stretch. He looked at her for a moment before walking over to stand before his students on the foul line. He wore a white knit shirt and creased white linen trousers.

Muti could not take her eyes from his tall, lanky frame. When he spoke to the boys she studied his sweet, gentle face. He smiled broadly as he greeted his students. Muti and Fariel's coach announced that they would work on their crosscourt backhands today. They took turns dashing from corner to corner of the court until they were breathless. Muti kept thinking of the deep cleft of Jag's chin, the glossy curl of his hair, still wet from his morning shower.

The class was a high intermediate level. Jag had told Muti she had potential to be an excellent player. Her own instructor said she was the best of her class, although the others had played for years, and she'd started only at the beginning of the school summer break. Muti thought it was her determination to run down every ball, no matter how impossible the get seemed, that made her a good player. Jag had said she was a natural with her muscular body and her athletic coordination. And quite apart from her attraction to Jag,

Muti loved the sport, the competition, the concentration and mental acuity it required.

Afterward Muti and Fariel ordered nimbu pani, and carried their sweating drinks to the risers near the white tent at the side of the court where the tennis pros kept their things. The sour of the barely diluted lime juice made Muti shiver, even in the humid monsoon heat. Muti waited until no one else was around, and ducked into the tent, leaving Fariel on the bleachers waiting for Moby, a club pro who was her cousin, and two girls from their tennis class. Fariel kept her eyes open for anyone headed for the tent while she and the others watched a match begin on the next court. Jag sat in a chair wiping his arms with a towel. Muti was relieved that he was alone. He had only a half-hour break, and they could talk without interruption.

"You were burning up the court today," Jag said. Muti felt heat rise in her throat and cheeks. "Where did you learn that backhand? It's as good as your forehand. I know you don't have anywhere else to practice. Really, Muti, you should be taking tennis more seriously."

"It's so much fun," she said, as Jag stood to pull a folding chair next to his wooden one. "I wish I could play all year."

"Well, maybe your family will reconsider," he said, draping his towel over his knees. "I'm sure you can be persuasive." She smiled, but didn't respond.

He leaned forward and took her hand and held it in both of his. She loved the feeling of their warmth and largeness.

"What are we going to do, my dear Mumtaz?" he asked.

"School starts in a couple of weeks," Muti said. "Jag, I

have to stop this. I . . . we can't take such a risk. You could lose your job, and I . . ." Jag's face didn't change, and she couldn't quite get out any more words.

"I was afraid you would switch off," he said quietly. "Why? Do you care about someone else?"

"Of course not!" Muti said, immediately lowering her voice again. "It's because I care too much about you. I'm afraid my aunt—my half sister—might persuade my uncle, my cousin, really, to send me back to the village. They'd marry me off to a country boy and I'd end up not finishing school, living in a dusty village for the rest of my life." Jag leaned forward and laid his hand along her jaw. With his thumb he wiped away a tear that had begun to roll down her cheek.

"We can't just not see each other," he said. "Maybe you underestimate your Uncle Omar. He has a reputation for being open-minded . . ."

"I don't know why," Muti said bitterly. "He came back from America to marry his cousin and take care of the family holdings. She tells him what to do all the time. When my grandfather—well, my uncle, really—is gone, he'll probably be the next leader of the Amirzai tribe. Baba is the one who understands me. They only let him get away with his modern ideas because he's an eccentric old man." Jag's eyebrows raised and lowered in confusion.

"Your family sounds as complicated as mine," he said, reaching for her other hand and holding them together in his. "Can you look at me and tell me seriously you're going to walk away from me?" he said.

Just then Fariel flipped open the tent-flap door. "Muti—your uncle's driver is here!"

Muti's heart lurched again. She squeezed Jag's hands, and stood abruptly.

"I've got to go," she said. He stood when she did. "If I can come before my lesson next week I will." The words were out of her mouth before she realized she'd just said goodbye to Jag, not one minute ago. Coming to her lesson next week—let alone before the lesson—would be impossible. Jag watched as she scooped up her racket and her duffel.

7

Jameel's mother looked up from her desk in the corner of the family room, where she was paying bills, and lifted one eyebrow.

"Well, Beta," she said with a half smile, "to what do we owe the honor?" *Beta* was the Urdu word for "son," and Jameel didn't like her to call him that. His mother was not like some Pakistani mothers, who could not see beyond the way things were done in Pakistan. But Jameel wanted to fit in, and when she called him Beta it reminded him of how different he was from the guys at Pier 7.

She usually called him Beta these days only when she was teasing. It was her way of asking what he was doing back so early from skateboarding. He sank down in the plaid easy chair nearest the desk.

"I have some things I need to do," he said.

"On your backside?" his mother asked. "In the easy chair?" He smiled despite a restlessness that made it difficult to keep from jiggling his feet. A moment later he stood and went to the kitchen and made a sandwich to take upstairs, where he sat at his own desk in the corner of his bedroom.

"Dear Muti," he wrote.

Jameel had lived in San Francisco his entire life. Every summer he and his parents went to Lahore. His father stayed two weeks, then came back to San Francisco to look after his medical practice. He didn't return until the last two weeks of the summer, after a quick stop in Karachi to see his parents. Jameel and his mother settled into the big, bustling household at Number 5 Anwar Road, where Jameel spent long days swimming with Muti and playing cricket with his cousin Jaffar. Sometimes Muti had played with them, but this year Auntie Leyla had made her stop. Often Baba took Muti, Jaffar, and Jameel to the farm at Okurabad, where they rode horses, swam in the irrigation canal that ran beside the garden gate, and toured the farmlands, which extended more than a day's drive by Pajero in every direction. Each evening they came back happy and covered in dust.

Muti was his closest friend in the world, and he wanted to tell her about almost kissing Chloe. It was too personal for an e-mail. And after the weirdness of Auntie Leyla watching every move they made and treating Muti like a servant, he didn't want to risk getting her into trouble. He missed Muti—he'd write her a letter and send it to Fariel so that Leyla wouldn't find it. But apart from "Dear Muti," he couldn't think what to say. Nothing had happened. He was stuck.

He stood and paced the room. He sat again and began on the body of the letter.

I wish you were here, Muti—I need help!!! I told you that I was falling for Chloe—that she's a good skateboarder, and that she's beautiful, which she is. Today she and I were the only ones at the pier. I almost kissed her. But—you won't believe this—I had this weird feeling, and all I could think of was my mother watching me!

He dropped the pen beside the pad of pale blue vellum and ripped off the top sheet, wadded it into a ball, and stuffed it into his pocket. Muti might think him stupid for imagining his mother watching.

Jameel spent the rest of the afternoon helping his mother empty the concrete planters along the driveway and replant them with mums and other autumn-colored flowers, ivy, and pale leafy things he couldn't identify.

As he worked, Jameel began to think of how stupid he'd been. It hadn't occurred to him that kissing Chloe would be so easy—so natural—but then, he'd never actually thought about kissing her before. At least, he didn't think he'd thought about it. But he could have—and why not? Would his mother and father really disapprove? And so what—whose parents wanted to see their son getting physical with a girl for the first time? And it was not as if they'd really seen him. He must be the only fifteen-year-old male in the world who'd ever stopped himself from kissing a girl because he imagined his mother was watching.

Just thinking what the guys at the pier would say made the tips of his ears glow. They'd never understand what being Pakistani was like—how much more protective his parents were than any of theirs. As for the idea of his falling for a blond chick who lived in the Tenderloin—he could just hear his parents scolding that she wasn't Muslim, that her background was too different, what would his grandfather think, and so on.

Jameel talked Asma into giving him an early dinner. She complained all the while she was setting the table. He sat at the kitchen bar and watched, only half listening as Asma rattled on about how one day he wouldn't eat anything, and the next day he wanted six meals. As Jameel's ayah, Asma saw herself as representing his parents when they weren't there. Asma had looked after him since he was a baby—she'd come with his parents to America before he was born. Jameel loved her almost as if she were his mother, but he bridled at her fussing over him. She, too, was a reminder of how different he was from his friends.

"Why don't you just let me eat here at the kitchen bar?" he asked, interrupting.

"You should eat at the table and behave properly," Asma scolded. She was a small, compact woman who wore a yellow cotton shalwar kameez. Her hair fell in a long braid, straight down her spine almost to her waist.

His mother and father were going out to the Indian Consul-General's house for dinner and the rest of the evening, which was the reason Jameel was eating alone. He waited until they were gone, and Asma was busy cleaning up the kitchen, before slipping out the back gate just as he had done that morning. This time he was not going to chicken out.

He loved dusk in San Francisco. The air was cool and clear and the lights came on one at a time, just the same way the stars came out, until the darkness was alive and shining.

Jameel arrived at the park to find all of the guys were there. "Hey, Osama!" shouted Cat. Jameel waved and dropped his board to the pavement. Dog Man and Slew Foot were demonstrating sequences of ollies, kick flips, and sex changes, their boards flipping, their bodies twisting, landing on their decks in fluid, feline movements. They kept it up until some of the guys got impatient and called them snakers for hogging the ramps.

On the other side of the ramps Chloe sat on her board, her back against the fence, watching. Jameel made his way over to sit beside her, and there were a few catcalls. "Who knew, Blue?" someone shouted. Chloe never gave any of these guys the time of day, so they had to make a big fuss when she let someone sit next to her, Jameel thought. She grinned up at him and scooted over to make room. Even in the klieg-lit glow around the park her eyes and hair were luminous. Jameel knew he'd been right to come back, and a thrill of well-being warmed him all over.

It was fun, hanging out with the guys, standing or sitting beside Chloe while they talked about who was going to the Radlands in England for the comp trials, and bragging about their moves, slams and all. It amused Jameel that Chloe never said a word or gave any indication she could outmaneuver all of them. She praised them and made them feel good. He wondered whether it was modesty—or perhaps that she didn't know how good she was.

When Jameel realized it was almost ten o'clock, he was anxious all over again. It was early to the skateboarders, but Jameel's parents would be worried if they got home and he wasn't there. He didn't want to just slip away, because he wanted Chloe to walk him out to the gate. He needn't have worried. When she saw him look at his watch, she tilted her head toward Embarcadero and said, "Come on, I'll walk you out. I need to get home early."

A few more catcalls followed them as they walked, and Chloe hooked her finger into the back pocket of Jameel's jeans. All of his consciousness seemed centered on the light pressure where her finger rested.

She was grinning broadly when they stopped at the traffic light on Broadway and Davis Street. When the light changed, Jameel slipped his arm around Chloe's shoulder, which fit neatly under his armpit as if they were built to fit together. They walked that way to the other side of the intersection. Jameel dropped his board on the sidewalk and held it there with one foot. With his other arm still around Chloe's shoulders, he pulled her closer and leaned toward her. He was startled at how soft her lips were and even more startled when he opened his eyes and saw she was watching him kiss her. He'd never in his life felt anything like that hot emptiness at the top of his stomach.

8

Muti made her way to the Old City by bus, jostling among merchants carrying rugs and bolts of cloth on their shoulders, darzis carrying sewing machines, children carrying bags of books, women with their shopping bags, all crushed together in the heat and murky humidity of a monsoon day. She got down from the bus at Circular Road, a thoroughfare that ringed the walled city with honking and clattering throngs of donkeys, buses, automobiles, handcarts, and brightly painted motor rickshaws. So far the rain had held off—but blue-gray clouds boiled across the sky, and Muti hoped she'd make it to the haveli before they poured their contents over the city.

Sweat trickled down her neck and back under the chador draped around her from her head to her feet.

Muti's mind was as jumbled as the streets. She thought of her last glimpse of Jag as she left through the tent flap beside the tennis courts at the Lahore Club. He stood very still, a damp towel hanging from his hand. His eyebrows were raised and his lips were parted as if he wanted to say something. He looked as sad as Muti felt. She had skipped her next tennis lesson. But she knew she must see him again before he returned to Delhi for the next school term. Her goodbye had been almost a promise to come again.

Baba's health also worried her. At times he seemed his old self, but his color was sometimes a grayish, lifeless hue that was very unlike his usual pink cheeks. He lapsed into periods in which he seemed barely to recognize anyone. His eyes were often uncharacteristically dull. Then he'd come to dinner alight with his normal good humor, roaring that he wanted ice cream for dessert.

And Muti hadn't heard a word from Jameel since he returned to San Francisco. Usually they wrote each other at least once a week. She told herself it wasn't jealousy exactly that pricked at her heart. She just didn't want this Chloe person to make Jameel forget about her and his family in Lahore.

And there was something about Auntie Selma's telephone call yesterday—it was very unlike the composed, straightforward Selma. Auntie had invited her for lunch, being peculiarly precise about the time. "You must be here by twelve sharp," Selma had said.

"For lunch?" Muti asked.

"Last I heard, that was the meal eaten in the middle of the day," Selma said. Muti laughed, but Selma didn't.

"Yes, Auntie," Muti said. "I'll be exactly on time, at twelve." Muti had wanted an invitation all these years that she'd lived at Number 5 Anwar Road. Why was now the right time? Odd or not, Muti looked forward to seeing her father's sister. She had happy memories of times at the haveli with her mother, going to the classroom in the old nursery on the second floor, where Samiya awaited them with books and blackboard, chalk and pointer, with reading lessons and discussions of so many things.

And Muti remembered playing hide-and-seek in the haveli with her little fawn, Choti. She was free to run with other children in the alleys of the old walled city, playing kickball and hiding games and eating mangoes in the hot weather, sitting with her cousins on the steps that led into the stone courtyard. She thought of the stories told by Auntie Selma of the days when she and her brothers Rahim, Mahsood, and Nazir walked to school together, and they scared her with stories about the djinn that lived in the house in Gulberg. Muti remembered flying kites from the rooftop of the haveli in celebration of Basant, the spring festival, children and grownups alike coating their kite strings with resin and glass and cutting down each other's prized paper kites, snagging them with tree branches and holding them hostage to fly another day. Muti and her mother watched the brilliantly colored paper battle in bright sunlight from the rooftop of the haveli.

Her stomach tightened when she remembered going to the Anarkali Bazaar with her mother to find fabric for her shalwar kameez when her mother decided she was old enough to wear pretty clothes. How she'd loved the eyelet shalwar kameez, and the lawn shifts the darzi had made from the fabrics she'd chosen.

Muti made her way to Akbari Gate, where the traffic condensed to a thick clot of bodies, and from there she followed a maze of ever-narrower lanes toward the great onion domes of the Badshahi Mosque. The rain came then, and the traffic neither slowed nor thinned, the vehicles slogging through what seemed like instant mud in the streets. Umbrellas went up, people put newspapers over their heads, but kept on, seeming barely to notice the sheets of water in the air.

Although she hadn't been to the haveli since she was five, Muti remembered exactly how to get there. She walked quickly down the familiar narrow lanes lined with small wooden houses with their doors open to let in air. She passed a woman washing a toddler in a plastic dishpan, and another braiding the hair of a bright-eyed little girl. Inside another doorway a woman was grinding spices with mortar and pestle. Muti paused before the haveli's ancient gates of unpainted wood and lifted the heavy metal ring to knock. A delicate, birdlike woman answered the door within a few seconds, and Muti recognized Samiya.

"Ah-salaam-aleikum!" said Samiya. "Can I help you?"

"Samiya!" she blurted. "It's me—Mumtaz!" Samiya stared at her for a few seconds, and a look of surprise passed over her face.

"You've grown into—a beautiful young woman!" Samiya stammered. "I would never have known you were that same knobbly-kneed little girl chasing after her pet fawn!" Muti laughed and they hugged each other. Samiya broke free and held Muti at arm's length, looking at her in wonder.

"Come in! Madame Akhtar told me you were coming—and still I didn't recognize you!" Muti followed Samiya into the foyer, with its marble floors and high ceilings, bits of carnelian and lapis cut into patterns of flowers set into the white plaster wall panels. Samiya led her straight ahead to the durbar, where her father had met with his constituents until late at night. Samiya left Muti there while she fetched Selma.

It seemed a long time before Selma appeared, an imposing figure in white, tucking thick strands of gray hair behind her ear as she came into the room. She held her arms wide for Muti, as she'd done when Muti was that knobbly-kneed child.

"Mumtaz," the older woman said softly as she stroked Muti's hair. "I feel as if it's been a century since I've seen you—a lifetime at least." Mumtaz pulled back and looked at her father's sister's face.

"But, Auntie," said Muti, "I just saw you two weeks ago! And we've lived nearly ten years in the same city and you've never invited me to visit you. I almost came on my own several times."

"And it's good you didn't," said Selma. "As I've told you, child, there has been a reason. A very important reason. But now the time is right, and I've got a huge surprise for you. More than a surprise, really . . ." Selma looked grave—not happy, as Muti imagined she should look if she was offering a surprise.

Muti felt a strange prickle skip across the back of her neck, like the sharp-clawed scratching of little mice. Selma took her by the hand and led her through the durbar, past the main hallway that led to the dining room, through the kitchen, and into a back hallway, where a heavy wooden door opened onto a wooden platform with a dark stairway rising above it in a musty, narrow passage. Muti hesitated and Selma squeezed her hand.

"I'll go first," said Selma. "There's nothing to worry about. I don't put a light in here because I don't want people to use this stairway. My own feet know every tread and every riser." Muti followed her, and the feeling of anxiety grew into a heavy pressure in her throat.

At the top of the stairs they came out into a courtyard that Muti remembered as being filled with tarpaulin-covered piles of buckets, discarded tools, and the debris of long-forgotten construction projects. The courtyard had been surrounded by rooms piled high with old furniture shrouded under dust-covers like ghosts from the past. Now the courtyard was swept clean and the junk piles were replaced by huge china pots filled with palms, canna lilies, anthurium, and fragrant ginger and gardenias. The rain still pelted down, but the sun was breaking through the clouds, so that Muti had to squint against the misty light. She put up her umbrella and the two of them hunched under it to cross the open space, which was covered with stone pavers. Clouds of steam rose and swirled around their feet.

Selma led her to the doorway of the beautiful hand-carved marble summer pavilion that stood in the center of the courtyard, and ducked through the entry first. Muti followed, and again her eyes had to adjust. A small figure stood in the middle of the spacious pavilion lit by the sun filtered through the intricate latticework of the screens that formed the walls. Muti took two steps forward.

"My Mumtaz," said Shabanu and held her arms open. Muti turned her head toward Selma, not quite believing her eyes and ears.

"Is it my mother?" she asked Selma, who nodded, her face opening in an encouraging smile. Muti looked back at her mother in disbelief, unable to move. For a moment she just stared.

"I've waited so long to see you," said Shabanu, moving toward her daughter. "I couldn't tell you I was here, and all the while I was living just to see you again." Muti couldn't find her voice and her feet felt planted in the stone floor. Shabanu approached her slowly and put her arms around Muti. "I've dreamed of holding you every minute since the last time," Shabanu said.

"I don't understand!" Muti said, unaware that tears streamed down her face. She stood rigidly and Shabanu continued to hold her. "You've been here all this time?" Muti asked. "And you let me believe you were dead?" She turned her head to look at Selma again. "Is this why the time was never right for me to come here?"

"We had to wait until you were old enough to understand," Selma said. "It was to protect both of you—but especially you, Mumtaz." Selma moved to an arrangement of low chairs and bolsters that were clustered around a red carpet handwoven in an intricate pattern. "Come. Sit. Samiya's bringing lunch here."

Muti hesitated, then moved to sit on one of the low Swati chairs without speaking. Selma lowered herself to the floor and leaned against a bolster. Shabanu took a chair facing both of them.

"I know this is difficult," Shabanu began. "But you must listen carefully and try to understand. It was out of absolute necessity that I've had to hide here all these years. I've wanted nothing more than to see you, but keeping you safe was more important." Muti nodded, and her mother went on.

"Do you remember when I left you with the old ayah Zenat? I went to see Auntie Zabo, and I told you I'd be back that same day?" Muti nodded. "That was the last time I saw you. That day Uncle Nazir kidnapped Auntie Zabo and me." She told Muti how Nazir had tried to force her to marry him, and how she and Zabo had escaped to Cholistan, where they were to live with Shabanu's Auntie Sharma.

"I planned to send for you, and we would all live together in the desert, and you would grow up as I did, loving the animals and your freedom."

She told of Zabo's death and how the keeper of the tombs at Derawar and his sister had helped her.

"Somehow the news reached Lahore that I had been killed. By then I realized I had to let everyone believe I was dead so that Nazir would not try to take revenge on me by harming you. If I still refused to marry him I believe he would have killed me," said Shabanu. "And I shudder to think of the ways he could hurt you, Mumtaz."

"Nazir lives like a hermit now," said Selma. "I don't know whether he's defeated, or perhaps just watching and waiting for a chance to take his revenge on your mother." Muti listened quietly as her mother spoke of the years locked away on the rooftop, and the importance now of Muti's keeping the secret as long as Nazir lived.

Samiya came and served them lunch, which sat untouched on the table in front of them. Muti had difficulty understanding what her mother said. Each sentence evoked a memory of the pain of losing her. It was hard to reconcile the mother she'd loved and mourned with this woman who told the story of fabricating her own death.

Muti felt as if the familiar pieces of her life were breaking apart and trying to rearrange themselves like a jigsaw puzzle that no longer fit together. When her mother finished speaking, Muti had so many questions to ask, but no voice to ask them with.

"Will you come with me to Cholistan, Mumtaz?" Shabanu asked. But Muti was lost in the swirling mists of her own thoughts and didn't hear her mother's question. "To visit my mother and father?" Shabanu explained that she'd sent a message by pigeon and that she hoped to go soon. "It will be a good way for us to get to know each other again," Shabanu said.

Selma had been sitting quietly, listening. "I will ask Baba's permission to take you to visit your mother's family," she said. "Your mother will go ahead of us to spend time with them alone first. Traveling with me will be perfectly safe, and I'm sure Baba will agree."

"When?" asked Mumtaz. "School starts soon . . ."

"We'll arrange it with Ibne," Selma said. "I am sending another pigeon to see if it's safe to talk by telephone."

"Will the trip be dangerous?" Muti asked. "Will Ibne keep it secret from Uncle Nazir?"

Shabanu sat up straight and looked her daughter in the eye. "Do you remember the wild desert birds in the cage of the veranda at your father's house in Okurabad?" she asked. "He kept me like one of those birds for seven years. And for the last ten years I've been a captive like the pigeons here." She motioned toward the screened enclosure that held the birds beside the pavilion. "I am still a wild desert bird, Mumtaz! I have come to feel I can no longer exist without seeing the dunes of the desert and its blue luminous stars. I cannot let fear keep me here any longer. And I can't let fear keep you where you are, with Leyla mistreating you."

Muti looked from her mother to Auntie Selma.

"Are you telling me I must come to Cholistan with you?" she asked. "And will we stay there? I thought you wanted me to go to school!" Muti thought of leaving Fariel, and St. Agnes Academy, and not spending summers with Jameel. These were the solid things in her life. "And how do I know you won't leave me again?"

Selma leaned forward and put her hands on her knees as if to rise. "Nothing has been arranged yet. Nazir is unwell, with no allies—a toothless tiger—and I don't think he has the means to harm you. We must be as sure as it's possible to be that we can do this safely, but we must act quickly. If the opportunity arose, Leyla would dispose of you like an old cabbage leaf, Mumtaz."

Muti nodded. She needed time to think about this. She felt very uncomfortable with her mother: part of her wanted to throw her arms around her and hold her forever, and another part of her wanted Shabanu to go away. The mixture of anger and love and fear that she'd be abandoned again and guilt and a kind of dislocation—as if time had reversed itself—lurched around in her mind, leaving her unable to trust herself to speak.

"I know," Selma said, struggling to her feet, "you need time to get used to this. But remember, Mumtaz, we want more than anything for you to be safe and happy. You have to trust us about that."

Muti left the haveli with her head feeling heavy. She paused a block away from the bus stop, traffic blaring in the street, pedestrians jostling her, and pirated CDs blaring from a shop next to her. Think of one thing at a time, she coached herself. And the first thought she settled on was Jag. She decided she must say goodbye to him properly so she might put him out of her mind. Perhaps then she would be better able to think more clearly about having a mother again.

Muti started with a more resolute step for the bus stop. She took a transfer for the Cantonment area. She sat in the women's section of the bus, and the tang of fresh vegetables from the bazaar mingled with the sweet smell of bodies doused liberally with talcum powder against the heat. She stood, her body swaying along with the bodies of other burqa-clad women, and fought her way to the exit door when the bus reached the Cantonment. She stood by the side of the road and hailed a motor rickshaw painted red and green and black with small silver chains and medallions hanging from the frame for its side curtains. She asked the driver to go to Mustafa Road, and pulled the side curtains around her. The rickshaw darted and swerved, lurched to a stop and started again with a jolt, its horn bleating like a distressed lamb. She paid the driver ten rupees and told him to keep the change. By the time the chowkidar swung the courtyard gate open, Mumtaz felt better.

"Hi!" Fariel said, opening the front door. "You're just in time for tea."

"Ummm," Muti said, not wanting to be rude. "D'you think we might go somewhere and talk?" Fariel looked over her shoulder.

"Are you all right?" she asked. Muti pressed her lips together and blinked back tears. "Please bring the tea to my room," Fariel said to the bearer, who nodded. Fariel linked her arm through Muti's and led her into the front hallway, where the children were coming in from play for their tea. The smell of curry pastries and sweet vanilla biscuits filled the air.

They sat in the little parlor area at the end of Fariel's bedroom. Like everything in the house, it was simple; the cover on her bed was rough homespun cloth in faded blue and white stripes and the curtains at her window were rough white homespun cloth. A dusty three-blade fan twirled lazily overhead. Muti was drawn in as always by the cool, calm openness and simplicity of the house and the people in it. She and Fariel settled onto floor cushions and leaned against bolsters, and Fariel poured green tea into delicate china cups.

For a moment Muti didn't know where to start. She couldn't tell Fariel about her mother, but she had to have at least one thing settled in her mind, and so she began with Jag. She told about her attempt to say goodbye to him, and remembering the sadness on his face brought tears to her eyes again.

"Muti, you must go back and say goodbye at least!" said Fariel. "I'm such a dummy—how could I not see how much you've grown to care for him?"

"It's all so hopeless," Muti said. "I guess I didn't want to admit how involved I was. But yes—I do want to say goodbye properly. Will you help me?"

Fariel nodded. "I have a lesson tomorrow morning. Want to come?" They agreed that Fariel and Shaheen would pick Muti up at nine o'clock sharp the next morning.

9

Muti sat under the pergola near the tennis courts at the Lahore Club sipping an icy nimbu soda. Fariel had just finished her lesson. Jag was not on the tennis court, nor was he in the tent where the coaches took their break. Fariel had gone off to see if she could find out where he was and when he'd be back.

Muti's drink sat before her on an old wicker table that seemed to be held together with white paint. She contemplated the ice that was nearly melted inside the glass, and the condensation that had pooled on the glass tabletop. Fariel burst around the corner of the clubhouse, startling Muti.

"Omar says Baba has fallen ill!" Fariel said, almost shouting. "He's here to take you to the hospital." Muti looked at Fariel as if she'd been speaking a foreign language. "Come on!" Fariel picked up her duffel and pulled on Muti's hand to heft her out of the chair.

"Did he say what's wrong?" Muti asked, rising from the

cushions and pulling back against Fariel's hand as if resisting would keep Baba from being seriously ill.

"I don't know—he didn't say." Fariel led her along the path from the tennis courts into the clubhouse.

"Oh, God help me!" Muti wailed. She stopped and covered her face with both hands. "It's my fault!"

Fariel looked back at her in amazement. "How could it possibly be your fault?" Muti was sobbing into her hands, the tears leaking out between her fingers. Fariel set down her duffel and put her arms around her friend.

"I knew something was wrong. He's stayed in bed every morning this week. Usually he's out of the house before the servants are awake. And sometimes he seems confused. I was thinking about saying goodbye to Jag and I was mad at Leyla because she has all these lunches and parties—and I'm the servant and—I wasn't thinking!" And since yesterday Muti had been so preoccupied with thoughts of her mother that she hadn't even thought once about how serious Baba's disorientation might be.

"Why should you have known?" Fariel asked.

"Baba has had headaches, and he looks terrible. Sometimes he's confused, but other times he's fine. Nobody seems to pay any attention. I mentioned it to Omar, and he said Baba is just getting old . . . But I should have known something was wrong. I couldn't bear it, if he . . ." She couldn't say what she feared. A silent prayer played through her mind, asking Allah to spare her baba, who was old and wise and fun-loving, a child in his heart that loved so deeply, who was incapable of speaking anything but the truth.

"Muti, you are not the adult in that house," Fariel said fiercely. She held on to Muti's hand and led her more gently down the path, which was shaded by palm trees and lined with ferns. Inside the clubhouse they blinked against the cool, dark calm of the reception lounge. They found Omar looking out through the large picture windows into the garden, his back turned to them.

"Omar?" Muti said softly, brushing the tears from her face. She hoped he would tell her that Fariel was mistaken, that Baba wasn't really ill, perhaps that he was only tired, or had a bout of indigestion. But when Omar turned toward her his face looked pale and he did not smile.

"Your baba had some kind of spell this morning, Mumtaz," he said, taking her by the shoulders. Omar spoke calmly, but Muti could see that he was extremely worried. She wanted to believe his voice, but she knew his face told the truth, and she could not keep a sob from rising through her throat. "Asrar is taking him to Jinnah Hospital now," Omar went on. "He's asleep, and we haven't been able to awaken him. When I telephoned Dr. Ghafoor he said it might have been a stroke. We'll meet them there."

"This is my fault," Muti said through her tears, which dripped now from her chin. "I should have realized he was sick. He hasn't been himself, and I should have insisted you take him to a doctor before this!"

"Nay, Mango," said Omar, circling her shoulders with his arm and drawing her toward the door. "You've been telling me for a week. Every morning I've phoned Leyla after I reach the office. Today she sent Asrar to Father's room to get him down for his breakfast. He woke up, but he wasn't feeling well. He bathed, and Asrar helped him down to the dining room. He was alone just while Asrar got his orange juice. He fell off his chair onto the floor, right there at the dining table. When Khoda Baksh and I got to the house, Father was awake. He asked to see you and Jameel. Then he went to sleep and we called the doctor, who said he'd meet us at the hospital."

While he talked, Omar guided Muti through the humid heat and bright, misty sunlight toward the car, steering her with his arm around her shoulders. Fariel followed behind.

"Is Jameel coming?" asked Muti, stopping halfway across the parking lot.

"I've telephoned Nargis in San Francisco," said Omar. "They're trying to get a flight. I told her I'd call later to see when they'll be here. We should know more then—perhaps Father will be better after he sleeps." Omar pulled her gently along. Muti still hung back, as if going to the hospital would make this real.

"Come, Fariel," said Omar. "We'll drop you at home."

Omar took Fariel's tennis bag and put it into the trunk of the car. Khoda Baksh's face was a blank mask. He had served as Baba's driver for many years. He and Asrar had been his faithful servants and confidants since Baba was a boy. Many evenings Baba had sat with Asrar, who was his secretary, and Khoda Baksh in the study, arguing about politics. Every once in a while one of them would smack the tabletop with the flat of his hand to make a strong point. Often laughter leaked through the keyhole and the crack under the door. They had been best friends as boys, when Khoda Baksh's father drove Baba's father and Asrar's mother had been Baba's ayah.

Muti and Fariel sat in the backseat, and Khoda Baksh and Omar sat in front. No one said a word as the car weaved its way through the traffic to the hospital. Muti felt as if her life was being pulled apart at its loosely stitched seams. Ever since she saw her mother the day before, she'd felt angry and depressed and guilty. Why couldn't she simply be filled with joy that her mother was alive? Why couldn't she feel safe finally—and be close to her mother as she had been when she was small?

And now Baba's falling ill and Leyla's threats to marry her away felt like a storm growing in her heart, which was seized by a fear she hadn't known in a long time.

Muti thought of Baba's kindness when she'd first come to Number 5 Anwar Road as a frightened orphan ten years before.

When she and Omar got out of the car after the long drive from Cholistan, Baba had been there to greet her. He spread his arms wide, and instinctively she ran to him. He'd scooped her up and twirled her around. It was the first time Muti had smiled since she and Omar had left the desert many hours earlier.

Baba often took her into his study while he worked, and placed photo albums in her lap, carefully turning the crumbling black pages. One album held photos of her father when he was a boy playing cricket with his brothers and cousins in the park near Shalimar Gardens. In an old photograph of Auntie Selma, their one sister stood tall and slim in a knee-length dress, one hand resting on the other arm, her dark hair curling down around her shoulders, her smile broad and filled with promise.

There were other albums with school photos and wedding photos, including one of Shabanu in a beautiful hand-embroidered shatoosh shawl. Her eyes were cast down and her mouth was set softly, pensively, unsmiling. When Muti saw this picture she remembered the special red-rose scent of her mother as she sat at her dressing table while the old ayah Zenat curled her hair with an iron heated in the fire.

Baba let Muti sit on his knee while he ate breakfast and lunch, sharing pieces of roti and bites of egg with her because she refused to eat otherwise. He taught her to ride the Arabian horses he kept in the stables at Okurabad by settling her into the saddle in front of him when he rode.

The reason Muti refused to eat when she was at Number 5 Anwar Road was that the women of the household—Leyla and her mother, Amina, and their servants—acted as if having Muti there was the most annoying aspect of their lives. When Baba wasn't at home they took her to the kitchen for the cook to keep an eye on her. They left her sitting on the floor, stepping around her, sometimes cursing under their breath when they tripped over her. The women never failed to remind her that she was alone in the world. Muti missed her mother, her father, and her mother's Auntie Sharma.

Muti tried not to cry when Leyla and Amina were nearby. One day she sat on a swing in the garden, where she picked small white flowers and braided them into a wreath. She had made halos for her mother of these same flowers at her father's farm. Remembering made Muti's eyes leak tears.

"Stop being a nuisance," said Leyla, who had come into the garden without Muti's hearing. "You have to get used to being here. And we have to get used to having you here. None of us has any choice."

Leyla refused to buy Muti new clothes. She and Amina would rummage through piles of clothing that had been discarded by their relatives to be taken to charity. "Your cousins hardly wore these," Leyla would say, holding up a mended shift and a shalwar with no matching top. And so when she was small, Muti wore clothes that were mismatched, or had been bleached to colorlessness in the laundry, dresses that were so large she tripped over them, or so short she had to pull at the hems to cover her legs.

From the beginning Leyla had made a fuss, insisting that Muti call her Auntie. She wanted her son, Jaffar, who was five years younger than Muti, to call her Madame instead of Mother. Between the photos in Baba's study and what Muti observed of the sometimes stormy relationships in the house at Number 5 Anwar Road, she slowly pieced together the relationships in this strange and unstable family.

Until Baba insisted the others treat her like an equal member of the family, Muti was allowed at the table only after everyone else had eaten, and was given their leftovers. Baba spoke sharply to Leyla for making Mumtaz clear the table after dinner.

"She is not your servant!" he had roared, drawing himself up to his full six feet. Leyla had looked stunned, but she did not reply. And from that time forward, Muti had not been forced to work in the kitchen or to serve at or clear the table unless Baba was not around or was too busy to notice. After that, Leyla and Amina devised and perfected the death by a thousand pinpricks, and Muti was made to look after the smaller children, deliver messages, and serve tea when Baba was not in the house. They let Muti know in every way they could that she was not their equal.

* * *

In the backseat of Omar's car, Muti's heart swelled with fear. She had always trusted Baba and Omar to take care of her. If Baba dies now, she wondered, will Omar stand up to Leyla? She could not imagine it. Omar was a conciliator, but without Baba, Leyla's power might grow.

That was the thing about being a captive bird, Muti thought. You learned to adapt, and before you knew it your captivity seemed normal. If you were free once again, you would become confused and miss the security of your captivity. For the first time since she'd seen her mother she felt the bonds of anger loosen around her heart. Next to her mother, no one had loved Muti the way Baba had—not even her father. But she wouldn't think about that now. She would concentrate instead on praying for Baba's recovery.

10

Jameel had no sooner pressed his lips against Chloe's than his cell phone began to vibrate in his pocket. He dropped his arms from around her and retrieved it, flipping open the cover, and the moment was totally gone.

"Yes, Mommy," he said softly into the phone, turning his back so Chloe couldn't hear. He'd always called his mother Mommy, but it occurred to him just then that it might sound childish. At first there was silence on the other end of the line, and then he heard his mother draw in a long, shaky breath. "What is it?" he asked.

"Where are you, Beta?" It sounded as if she'd been crying. "I'm sending Javed for you immediately." Javed drove Jameel's father to work, then came back to drive his mother to the market and on other errands around San Francisco. Javed had taken them that evening to the Indian Consul-General's house.

"Tell me what's wrong!" He kept his voice low. His

mother was usually calm and reserved. She was not like some other Pakistani-American mothers: overprotective, disapproving, and subject to panic at the most normal things.

"We're on our way home. It's your grandfather," she said. "We're leaving for Lahore on the first flight we can catch. We have to—"

"What's happened?" Jameel asked. "Is he . . ."

"It sounds as if he's had a stroke, Beta," she said. "He's in and out of consciousness. It sounds very bad. I want to see him . . . well, as soon as possible. Before he went unconscious he was asking for you. Uncle Omar says we must come now. We're on standby for a flight that leaves around noon tomorrow. I'll pack your things and we must get some sleep."

"Tell Javed to meet me at the corner of Embarcadero and Broadway," Jameel said quickly. "I'm going there right now."

Jameel folded his cell phone and dropped it back into his pocket. He flipped his skateboard with his toe, caught it, and held out his hand to Chloe.

"I have to go," he said, his face coloring. She held on to his hand.

"I know, Jimmy," said Chloe. "I heard."

"It's my grandfather," Jameel said quickly. His throat tightened and he was embarrassed to feel the pressure of tears behind his eyes. Chloe squeezed his hand. "He's, he's . . . It sounds bad. He's in a hospital in Lahore. We're leaving tomorrow." Jameel felt a little faint. The edges of his vision darkened and telescoped inward. Chloe shook his arm.

"Jameel—what's wrong?" She led him by the hand to a concrete bench near a bus stop and guided him to sit on it. "You look as if you've seen a ghost! You're sweating."

Jameel's vision cleared and he took deep breaths until his head stopped doing loops. Chloe was wiping his forehead and face with a red bandanna kerchief doused with cool water from her bottle.

"My grandfather and I have always been very close. I'm named for him—Mahsood Jameel is my real name, just like his: Mahsood Jameel Muhammad Amirzai. They called him Mahsood, except for my grandmother, who called him Jameel. He's always been so healthy, and I guess I thought he'd live forever."

"Oh," she said. "I'm so sorry." Her eyes were round and her face was uncharacteristically still. She really was sorry, Jameel thought. She handed him her water bottle. "Here—you probably should drink this." He obeyed.

"Thanks," he said. "Chloe, I . . ." To Jameel's horror his throat closed and he felt tears prickling again at the back of his eyes.

"Are you okay?" she asked. He nodded and turned his head to swipe at the tears with her kerchief. She turned, so he could see her face fully lit in the streetlight.

"I don't pray very often," she said, "but I'll pray for him. And I'll think about you and send you good thoughts. I'll do it at eight every morning so you can be listening." Her blue eyes clouded for a moment. "Will a Jew's prayers work?"

Jameel cleared his throat and managed to smile. "Muslims and Christians and Jews all pray to the same God, Chloe.

Yes, they'll work just fine. At eight every morning. That will be eight at night in Pakistan," he said. "I'll be there when you are. Chloe . . . I'm so glad . . ." He wasn't sure what to say she was—his girlfriend? That seemed a little extreme.

She smiled and leaned forward to plant a kiss softly on his mouth. "Me too," she said. He was surprised and couldn't speak for a moment. The kiss stayed right there on his lips, where she left it. He smiled back at her and they both stood. Chloe hooked her finger into his back jeans pocket again as they walked toward the corner where Javed would meet him.

"Thanks, Chloe," he said a few minutes later when the black Mercedes rolled up to the stoplight on Broadway, a block away. "I'll see you soon." Jameel felt a stab of embarrassed alarm as they approached the car, but Chloe didn't even seem to notice. She took his hand and squeezed it quickly before letting go.

"Bye, Jimmy," she said, her voice a soft whisper. He felt her eyes on his back all the way to the car, until he opened the rear door and climbed inside. He waved at her through the dark-tinted rear window. She probably couldn't see him, he thought, but she smiled and waved, then waved with her red kerchief so he could see her under the streetlight until the car turned the corner.

Jameel felt as if a giant fist had him by the heart, it thrashed and hammered so hard inside his chest. He wondered what it felt like, this sleep after a stroke—was it dark? Or just like sleeping? Or death, for that matter—would his grandfather be aware as he died that he was leaving all of those who loved him? He wondered if Grandfather was trying desperately to awaken. Jameel hadn't thought of these things when Grandmother had died the year before. He rested his head against the white linen cover on the backseat of his father's car as Javed drove along Embarcadero, passing warehouses with metal roofs that glinted dimly behind the streetlights.

Jameel closed his eyes, and an image popped into his head of himself and his grandfather riding the bright red-and-silver BMW motorcycle one July day through the streets of Gulberg near Number 5 Anwar Road. His grandfather whooped like a small boy, his white beard flying over his shoulder, just as it had on the Jet Ski this summer. Jameel held on for dear life, but he laughed the whole time as the wind snatched away his breath.

When Jameel got home it seemed every light in the house was lit. Upstairs his mother rushed back and forth from the laundry to his room. A large leather suitcase lay open on his bed, and a metal trunk sat on its end near the bedroom door.

"How long are we staying?" Jameel asked as she brushed past him with another armload of neatly folded shirts. When she didn't answer, Jameel followed her back to the laundry. She stopped beside the dryer and he ran into her.

"I don't know," she said, turning and stepping around him.

"But you don't have to pack *all* of my clothes—school starts in two weeks . . ."

"Jameel," she said, "I'm sorry—I don't know how long I should be packing for. I'm just trying to do it. Javed's getting gas in the car—he'll be back in a few minutes. Daddy's packing some papers in the office. Your grandfather is very ill. We don't know if he will live until we get to Lahore, or if he does, how long he'll be alive. Uncle Omar said the doctors don't know exactly what's wrong yet. They don't know whether he'll awaken again, so we can talk to him." She laid her hand against Jameel's cheek and then resumed bustling and looking worried.

11

When Muti and Omar arrived at Jinnah Hospital, they rushed to the second floor, where they found several relatives standing in a knot and talking quietly near the foot of Baba's bed in a large, dimly lit room. Nazir was there, and Auntie Selma, as well as various cousins. Only Selma stood near Baba, who lay under a sheet that was neatly tucked around him. Selma's hand rested on her brother's shoulder, and she talked gently to him as if he were awake. Nazir and two cousins stood apart from the others, their backs to the bed. A glucose drip was fastened to Baba's arm and his face was peaceful. Dr. Ghafoor came in and spread his arms as if to embrace them all.

"Please," said the doctor, "please take seats in the visitors' lounge. It's just across the hall. We don't know whether he will awaken, but if he does, the room shouldn't be so chaotic." One by one they moved quietly out into the hall, where they stood near the doorway as if reluctant to miss the old man's awakening. A fan clicked overhead, and a strong scent of antiseptic barely disguised the underlying smell of body fluids.

Dr. Ghafoor stopped Muti and Omar at the door and motioned for them to stay. Selma stayed behind, too.

"Is your nephew coming?" Dr. Ghafoor asked Omar. "You said he asked for his grandson and his niece."

"This is Mumtaz," said Omar. "It's the middle of the night in California, where Jameel and his family live. They were trying to get a seat on a flight that leaves around noon their time, I think. How much time does he have?" Mumtaz looked anxiously from Omar's face to the doctor's.

"There's no way to tell," Dr. Ghafoor said. "His vital signs are relatively weak. That could change. Right now the trend is toward further weakening. There's no way to know—it could be days, or a matter of hours. While it's possible that he'll awaken, you shouldn't have false hope. But it would be very good to have everyone he asked for here."

Muti had never seen Omar so shaken. His face was pale and droplets of sweat stood out on his forehead. "Please, Doctor, tell me the truth. Is there any chance my father will live?"

"I have told you the truth," said Dr. Ghafoor. "It appears he has had a cerebrovascular accident, most likely a thrombosis, a blood clot that has lodged in his brain. While he has weakened since he came in, it's possible that if he regains consciousness in the next twenty-four hours, he could survive. I suggest those of you who are closest to him take turns staying here with him. We don't know what role the will plays in surviving an event like this—if it's so important to him that he should talk with your niece and nephew, he may fight hard until Jameel arrives, and perhaps he'll regain consciousness."

"Can he hear if we talk to him?" asked Muti.

"Of course, we're not certain what a stroke patient can hear when he's in a coma. But nothing will be lost if you try, and a great deal might be gained."

Omar pulled a chair up to the bedside and beckoned Muti to sit. Muti reached under the cover for Baba's hand. It was warm and soft and very much alive. Muti squeezed her fingers around the huge palm, but his fingers did not return the pressure. She stroked his arm and looked into his face. His winged black eyebrows, which had always wriggled with pleasure when he smiled, were still.

"I'll check back in a while," said Dr. Ghafoor. "Send someone for me at once if he awakens."

Omar and Muti took turns talking to Baba, telling him that Jameel would soon be on his way, that the others were waiting outside, and how everyone was praying for his recovery. Selma stroked her brother's arm and talked softly near his ear. Omar and Selma began to reminisce, with Selma sitting in the chair next to the bed and Omar standing on the other side. Muti stood beside Omar and listened.

Across the hallway, Muti saw Uncle Nazir staring straight ahead into Baba's room. A memory of something so painful that Muti hadn't thought of the event since it happened flew into her mind with such unexpected ferocity she felt as if she'd been hit in the stomach.

It was on the farm at Okurabad, at a time when she felt happy and secure. She and her mother lived in a small mud brick building of one room across the stable yard from the kitchen. Her mother had declined to live in the big house, where her father lived with Amina and his other two wives and their children. Shabanu shielded Muti from the other women in Rahim's household.

One day when Muti was five, she was playing in the courtyard with her fawn, which she and her mother had named Choti because the deer remained little even as she matured. The fawn was a gift from her father. Shabanu and Muti had tied a red cord around Choti's neck with a little bell on it so Mumtaz could keep track of her pet. The ayah called Muti in for her lunch and a nap. Mumtaz had fallen asleep, as she always did, with Choti curled up beside her bed, her velvety nose buried between her delicate fawn legs.

When Mumtaz awoke, the fawn was not there. She and her mother searched all through the heat and dust of the afternoon. They looked in the kitchen, where the khansama sometimes slipped treats from the oven to Mumtaz when no one was watching; they walked along the canal, calling into the woods and underbrush; they searched the stables, where Choti was forbidden to go. By the end of the afternoon they still had not found the fawn.

The next morning Mumtaz awoke before her mother and slipped away to help the mali water the flowers and feed the birds in cages on the veranda of the big house. She hoped the mali might have seen Choti. On her way to the front garden, Mumtaz passed the courtyard in front of the garage, and there, hanging from a thick tree branch by their hind legs, were four deer, blood dripping in dark red ribbons from their noses. An indentation in the smallest doe's fur around the neck where the bell cord had hung identified Choti.

Mumtaz had run crying to her mother. Shabanu's lovely face turned pale and her eyes were like stones. She took Muti away to Lahore. And shortly afterward Rahim was killed in a dispute with Nazir over land. And not long after that, Shabanu was gone, too.

12

At Number 5 Anwar Road the silver tea service gleamed on the marble kitchen tabletop beside a butter cake under a blue-screened dome to keep away the flies. Leyla had spoken to Omar, and his father was settled at Jinnah Hospital. She was able to stay at home to get things ready for her luncheon. This time the occasion was her mother's birthday. She called her Aunt Tahira to tell her about Baba's illness.

"He has fallen ill before, Auntie," Leyla said. "These spells have landed him in the hospital three times. He stays up till all hours of the night gossiping with Khoda Baksh and Asrar—what do they think? That they're still boys? The hospital probably will phone at noon, just when everyone has arrived for a nice afternoon, and tell us to come and get him. Mark my words. Oh well. Khoda Baksh can bring him home."

"Shouldn't we go to the hospital and see him?" asked Auntie Tahira. "Perhaps we should postpone the party . . ."

"There is no need to put off the party," said Leyla. "He's tired, and he'll be fine once he's rested up. Everything is ready. I'm just waiting for Mumtaz to come and help. Just come at eleven-thirty, as planned."

Leyla tried Muti's mobile phone to check and see the girl hadn't forgotten to come home early to help with lunch. Where was she? She was so irresponsible. Leyla would have to talk to Omar again about marrying Mumtaz off. She was an embarrassment, and Leyla was certain she'd bring disaster down on the entire family if they continued to spoil and indulge her. The old man even encouraged her to think she was as good as Leyla and her sisters and cousins. That in itself could not have any good result.

The call from the hospital came earlier than Leyla had predicted. At 11:38, as she and Amina greeted Tahira and her daughters and grandchildren in the front hall, Omar telephoned. But what he had to say was not what Leyla expected.

"Dr. Ghafoor says he cannot predict whether or when Father will awaken," said Omar. "He believes his chances of regaining consciousness are better sooner, rather than later. He also thinks that if we stand beside him and talk to him he might hear us on some level. Mumtaz is here with me. Father also has asked for Jameel. I've spoken to Nargis and they're trying to get a flight. Will you please keep trying Nargis?"

"I have company coming for my mother's birthday. Auntie Tahira is already here." There was no answer from Omar's end of the line. "Omar, do you hear me? I can't be on the telephone all day. And Mumtaz is supposed to be here helping."

"I can't have my mobile on in intensive care," Omar said, exasperation in his voice. "Just please try San Francisco. They must get here before . . ." He stopped and Leyla sighed.

"Oh, all right. I'll try. Hold on." With her other hand she picked up her mobile phone and punched in the number for Nargis in San Francisco. He was trying her patience.

"It's busy," she said. It didn't occur to her to try Nargis's cell phone.

"You should send Tahira and your mother to the hospital," Omar said. "Father asked for Jameel and Mumtaz. And now he's in a coma. This is serious. He may not recover."

"But it'll ruin my mother's party!" Leyla said. "I have a houseful of people coming!" As they talked, Leyla tried Nargis's number again on the mobile phone. Still busy. "They're on the phone."

"Keep trying her mobile phone, please. It's almost midnight there—they're probably trying to get on a flight," said Omar. "And, Leyla, I insist that you stay by the telephone until you reach Nargis. You should send the others to the hospital."

"As you wish," she said, and hung up. Leyla tried once more to reach Nargis, but this time there was no answer. In San Francisco, Jameel and his parents had left a message on Omar's cell phone and finally had switched off their phones to get some sleep.

"Nargis is as unreliable as Mumtaz," Leyla muttered under her breath. "Unreliable in every way." Leyla sent Spin Gul, the second driver, to find her son, Jaffar, who was playing cricket in the maidan next to the canal. Since Omar insisted, she had no choice but to postpone her mother's birthday luncheon after all. When Jaffar arrived with his trousers grass-stained and dusty, sweat on his face and arms, Leyla clicked her tongue.

"Go!" she shrilled, her tension mounting by the minute. "Wash your face and hands. Change your shirt. You're as disreputable as your cousin." Jaffar cocked his head.

"She's not my cousin," Jaffar said, heading off obediently to the bathroom. "She's my aunt." Jaffar could tell by the petulant set of his mother's mouth that he'd best do as she asked without argument.

Leyla thought she might as well make the most of the situation. If she had to waste the afternoon by the telephone, it was better that Auntie and her cousins and nieces and nephews should not be left here waiting for her. And once she got to the hospital it would have been unpleasant to have to sit there all alone. Auntie Tahira had kept her car and driver.

The sandwiches, cakes, and tea were forgotten, and everyone piled into the two cars, Tahira and her daughter squeezed into the back of her car with four children, and Amina in the other car, driven by Spin Gul, with Jaffar in front beside Spin Gul.

Leyla did not like being left behind. She went into the house to put away the food and the silver tea service and to try telephoning Nargis again. But when she got to the kitchen, the marble-topped table was bare. She went to the fridge, and inside were the sandwiches and cakes, all wrapped in waxed paper and stored in plastic boxes. The inside of the refrigerator glowed with a strange bluish light, although the lightbulb was burned out. The ayah was off for the day, visiting relatives in University Town, and Leyla didn't know where the lightbulbs were kept.

Leyla heard the heavy front door slam, vibrating the windows in their frames. She went out into the hallway to find the front door shut and locked—just as she'd left it after saying goodbye to her mother and Auntie Tahira as they left for the hospital.

Leyla was not one to be frightened, but she was growing perturbed. Someone was obviously playing tricks. She unlocked the front door and walked out onto the veranda. The front gates were closed, but she was sure she would find the guards outside, napping in the guardhouse. In one furious movement she threw back the bolt and flung open the gates. The guards were at attention, and turned their starched gray turbans and turned-up mustaches toward her in amazement.

"Is something wrong, memsahib?" asked one.

"Did you see who came through these gates?" she asked.

"No one did, memsahib." They both shook their heads.

13

By late afternoon, Baba's grand-nieces and -nephews grew restless. Their mothers and ayahs kept them outside the hospital, where the boys played cricket and the girls sat under a tree serving each other tea. But there were only small, flat stones for teacups, and they soon grew tired of pretend cakes when they had been promised sandwiches and real butter cake at Auntie Leyla's.

Well past teatime, Amina and Tahira decided to take the children back to Number 5 Anwar Road. They had been fed biscuits and cold tea from a hamper the khansama had prepared, but these were small compensation for the missed sandwiches and butter cake, and by four-thirty they were irritable.

Selma had watched her brother Nazir from the other side of the visitors' lounge. He sat alone, like a small island amid a sea of male relatives who spoke in low tones about politics and cricket matches. But his appearance had changed since

Selma had seen him two weeks earlier at Number 5 Anwar Road. His hair and beard were neatly trimmed. He wore a fine silk vest over a white shalwar kameez. He was motionless in his chair, his face impassive, his hands hanging limply at the ends of his wrists over the wooden arms of the chair. He looked more alert—as if someone or something had shaken him out of a long sleep.

Selma wondered whether Nazir thought he was next in line for the tribal leadership when Mahsood was gone. Despite Mahsood's tendency to behave as if he thought he'd live forever, Selma felt certain her brother had a plan for his succession, and she was certain it would not include Nazir, even though he was the last surviving brother.

Selma rested in a chair in the visitors' lounge for a while, crossing the hall to sit with Baba so Mumtaz could get up and stretch. Baba's old friend and spiritual adviser, Maulvi Inayatullah, came and stood beside Baba's head. Gently he reached out and turned Baba's head to one side so that it would face Mecca. Inayatullah wet a cloth with water from a jar and wiped Baba's face with it. Muti looked up at Selma.

"Inayatullah has brought Zamzam water from the Holy Mosque in Mecca," Muti said. Inayatullah murmured a prayer as he worked. When he had finished, he stood back to make a space for Selma, who took the cloth and continued to stroke Baba's arms and face with it. Mumtaz took only a short break, and when she returned, Selma gave her her seat back and returned to the waiting lounge across the hall. She noticed that Nazir was gone.

Mumtaz also had noticed when Nazir slipped away. She'd always been aware, without knowing specifically why, that he was the family outcast—even more of an outcast than she was. He had small, mean eyes, and Muti had always felt uncomfortable around him. At family gatherings she'd sometimes caught him staring at her. When her eye caught his he didn't look away. Now she thought of him as the tiger Auntie Selma spoke of—not a toothless tiger, but one that sits quietly watching its prey.

Dr. Ghafoor stopped outside the waiting room a while after the others left. "Can I have tea sent to you?" he asked politely. Selma stood.

"I'm his sister," she said in her rich, husky voice. "Can you tell me anything? I don't want to leave if there's any chance he'll awaken." Dr. Ghafoor shook his head.

"He's been stable now for a couple of hours. That may be a sign he'll make it through the night. But it's impossible to say with any certainty." Selma nodded and rearranged her white lawn dupatta around her face. She crossed the hall to look down at her brother in the bed. He had not moved of his own will or changed his expression in the many hours she'd been there.

"I'll go home now and eat something," she said to Muti and Omar. "I'll sleep for a few hours, and come back so you two can get some rest."

"Why don't you get a good night's sleep and come back early tomorrow?" Omar said. "I'll telephone you if there's any change at all. Leave your phone by the bed."

Muti had always suspected her aunt came infrequently to

Number 5 Anwar Road because she was repelled by the currents of tension that ran through everything that happened in the house. Now she realized the irregularity of Auntie Selma's visits had to do with the secret she had kept for ten years. Muti used to think that perhaps she might stay with Auntie Selma if something happened to Baba and life at Number 5 Anwar Road became unbearable without him there to keep the pinprick level in check.

Omar went to the other side of the bed where Selma stood, and kissed her softly on the cheek.

"Unless I hear from you, then, I'll come back early in the morning," she said.

Mumtaz walked down the hall with her aunt. They said little until they reached the stairwell. Mumtaz turned to Selma. "I can't go to Cholistan with my mother," she said. "Will you tell her for me?" Selma took her arm and held on to the railing with the other hand as she went slowly down the stairs.

"Don't worry about your mother," she said. "You have enough on your mind at the moment."

"I don't want to hurt her," said Mumtaz when they reached the bottom of the steps. "And I'd like to see my grandparents. But I need to get used to the idea that she's here—that I have a mother!" Muti always remembered her grandparents as she'd left them standing side by side in the desert as they said goodbye to her. "Would it be all right if I went to Cholistan a little later?"

"Let us see what happens," Selma said, taking Muti's hands. "You are a good and strong girl, Mumtaz. You will get used to the idea, and you and your mother will find a way to be close again. She's having difficulty, too, having to adjust to knowing you're no longer a child."

Muti kissed her aunt, then hurried back upstairs to Baba's bedside. Soon she was engrossed in telling Baba everything she remembered about first coming to Number 5 Anwar Road. She didn't notice Maulvi Inayatullah praying at the foot of the bed or Omar leaving to use his mobile phone outside. When Omar came back he touched her gently on the shoulder.

"I've just spoken with Nargis," said Omar. "They'll be on a flight that leaves in a few hours. They'll be here tomorrow, after midnight." Muti's heart skipped a beat. Until that moment she had believed Baba would recover, but if Jameel was really coming from America, she thought, it meant they believed Baba was about to die.

Dr. Ghafoor appeared in the doorway. Omar shook his head in answer to the doctor's unasked question. Muti looked up and saw that the light had faded from the room's fly-specked and bird-splattered window. A nurse brought a lamp and plugged it into a wall socket. They had turned off the overhead light because it was too harsh. The nurse also brought a second chair, which Omar placed on the side of the bed opposite where Muti sat stroking Baba's hand and talking to him.

Muti didn't notice when Baba's breathing slowed and became shallower. His cheeks grew pale and his features sharpened. Omar sat across the bed from Muti, staring up at the ceiling.

Dr. Ghafoor came and went, but Mumtaz never paused in her detailed recital of the events of her life. She told Baba things she didn't even know she knew, much less remembered: how her mother had not wanted to marry her father; in the end her father had sent his faithful servant Ibne to fetch her on his magnificent white stallion; how her mother had fled with Zabo to the fort at Derawar. She talked as if she was in a trance, and she talked without ever repeating herself.

* * *

Baba did survive the night, and when Muti realized it was morning her hopes that Baba would recover soared. Auntie Selma came back looking as if she hadn't slept at all, and stood beside Muti's chair.

"You really must get some rest," Selma said to Muti. The nurses showed her to a small, bare room with a cot, and Muti lay down. She slept without dreaming for several hours. Someone had pulled a shawl over her, and she awoke not knowing where she was. And then she remembered. She looked at her watch. It was late afternoon. She rose and walked quickly down the hall to Baba's room. There she found Omar sitting with his head in his hands, a hamper of food at his feet. Selma sat beside Baba, talking gently to him.

"You should eat something," Selma said, lifting her eyes to Muti's briefly when she entered the room. "Nothing has changed."

Mumtaz reached into the hamper that Khoda Baksh had

brought from Number 5 Anwar Road and selected a limp chicken sandwich wrapped in waxed paper from Leyla's canceled luncheon the day before. She nibbled at it tentatively. It was soggy and stale, and she bolted down the rest of it to get something into her stomach. She poured some tea from a thermos into a cup and sipped it. It was still hot. She felt better.

Dr. Ghafoor came in and listened to Baba's heartbeat, then read the monitor that recorded his breathing. When the doctor was finished he straightened and turned to Selma, Omar, and Mumtaz.

"His pulse is very weak," he said. "His breathing is very shallow. There isn't much time . . ."

Nobody said anything, and the doctor folded his stethoscope into his pocket and left the room. The three of them took turns sitting with Baba, keeping watch. From time to time Omar left to use his telephone. Muti lost all track of the passing hours.

Late in the evening Muti awoke. She hadn't realized she'd fallen asleep with her head resting on Baba's arm. Selma slept in a chair in a corner of the room. Omar was asleep in the chair across the bed.

The hospital was still and quiet, and Muti was sure that Baba's voice had awakened her. She had the strange sensation that she was still sleeping, but she shook her head and tried to remember. What he'd said was "I cannot wait. You must do as I ask, child. All will be well."

At about the same time she became aware that the hand she held had grown cool. She looked up and Omar was alert across the bed from her. Something had awakened him, too. Maulvi Inayatullah had come in from the lounge across the hall. They all understood immediately. Omar placed his hand on his father's chest, but felt no heartbeat, no slight motion of lungs expanding to fill and contracting to exhale. Inayatullah moved to his old friend's side and gently reached out to touch Baba's closed eyes.

Omar ran to the doorway and called for the doctor, who came into the room some minutes later, fitting the wires of his spectacles over his ears. Dr. Ghafoor placed his stethoscope on Baba's chest and leaned over his body, his head turned to one side as he listened for a heartbeat. Muti focused on the dark haze of beard that covered Dr. Ghafoor's cheeks and repeated a prayer over and over: *Let Baba come back*. When the doctor finally straightened he shook his head.

"He just slipped away," said Muti, through tears that closed her throat and ran down her face. "I just noticed he'd grown cooler."

The doctor pronounced Baba dead at eleven o'clock in the evening.

Khoda Baksh had been keeping watch in the hallway outside his old friend's hospital room on the second floor. He had left the chowkidar at the hospital gate in charge of the car. He slept sitting upright on the floor, his back against the wall of the hallway, and was awakened by quiet shuffling in the room across from him. The light was shining beside the bed, and a nurse was pulling a sheet up over Mahsood Jameel Muhammad Amirzai's head. Mumtaz wept quietly in the chair beside him, the end of her dupatta pressed over her mouth. Selma stood beside her, one hand on Muti's shoulder. Omar was in the chair in the corner of the room, talking to Selma.

"The funeral will be tomorrow," he said, his voice weary. "Will you take care of the food? Leyla is at home. In the morning, after people are awake, she'll do some telephoning, along with Asrar. Khoda Baksh will drive Asrar and me to the airport in a little while to pick up Nargis, Tariq, and Jameel. Their flight arrives around one-thirty a.m. If you can't reach me on my mobile, try Leyla."

After all the time they'd spent watching over Baba as he lay in the hospital bed, it seemed strange that his body lay there, but he was no longer in it. After a while they went their separate ways: Selma to the haveli, and Omar and Mumtaz to Number 5 Anwar Road.

In the car Mumtaz felt Omar's eyes on her. They both sat in the backseat. She looked up, and he started to speak but couldn't find the words for what he wanted to say. She'd noticed just before they left the hospital that his face looked older by ten years than it had a day earlier, when she'd said goodbye before going off with Fariel in the morning.

"I'm so sorry, Omar," she said. He put his hand over hers on the seat between them.

"Mumtaz, I heard what you told my father," he whispered. "Is it true? Your mother is alive?" In the light from the streetlamps his eyes looked like black holes in a pale mask. Muti looked at Khoda Baksh in the rearview mirror to see whether he'd heard, but his eyes were on the road and she realized Omar had spoken so softly she'd barely heard his words.

"You told Baba," he said. "I heard you. Is it true?"

Muti couldn't think what to say. She didn't remember telling Baba, but how else would Omar know? She couldn't lie to him, but she'd promised her mother and Auntie Selma she'd never tell—she'd meant to keep the secret as faithfully as they had. Still, if there was anyone she could trust . . .

She pressed her lips together and nodded. When she looked at Omar again, she could see light reflecting from tears that streamed down his face. Mumtaz leaned toward him.

"She's lived with Selma all this time," Muti whispered. "I didn't know. I'll tell you the rest—but we must keep her secret. Please help me!" Omar nodded and closed his hand over hers.

"After I drop you at home there will be no time," he said. "I must know now." His voice came out in a harsh whisper. Mumtaz explained quietly how her mother had allowed her—all of them—to believe that she was dead to protect herself and Muti. When she'd finished, Omar looked out the window and they didn't speak again for the remainder of the ride home.

14

Jameel sat in the window seat of a row in the business-class section of the jetliner bound for Pakistan. They had made stops in Toronto and Manchester, and had been traveling for more than twenty hours. Jameel's father sat beside him, and his mother was in the aisle seat. Three plastic cups filled with orange juice sat untouched before them on fold-out trays. Cabin attendants seemed to glide up and down the aisles, bending to spread stiff white linens on the trays and distributing little packets of plastic forks and knives. The yeasty, salty smell of mushrooms for business-class omelettes emanated from the galley, making Jameel's stomach churn.

Every year when Jameel and his parents made this same journey, Jameel felt that the airplane was traveling backward in time, as well as narrowing the distance between his home in San Francisco and his mother's family home in Lahore. Especially when they visited his grandfather's ancestral home in Okurabad, Jameel felt as if he was in a time warp. All of the Amirzai lands centered around Okurabad, where things hadn't changed much in the last five hundred years. In Lahore, Jameel and his parents behaved more formally than they did during the rest of the year in California. It was almost as if they'd entered the Victorian era when they came to Lahore. Jameel felt caught somewhere between out of place and comfortable in both cities.

Jameel's father sat tight-lipped, staring straight ahead. Jameel wondered what went on behind his fixed and troubled eyes. He knew his father and grandfather had not always seen eye-to-eye. His grandfather was reluctant to admit that anyone was good enough to be married to his daughter, even after all this time. And Jameel's father, Tariq, bridled when Nargis insisted they spend most of every summer holiday with her father, rather than with Tariq's family, who lived in Karachi. By custom in Pakistan, the husband's family had first consideration. But they had not lived in Pakistan since shortly after their marriage sixteen years earlier. Despite Tariq's resentment he found the old man charming, and his progressive views on Islam and Pakistan interesting. Gradually Baba had won him over.

Tariq and Baba had come to love each other in the involuntary way that tends to glue together family members for whom it might be more comfortable to grow apart.

Jameel was relieved that his parents seemed not to require him to participate in a conversation. His mother reclined her seat, pulled an airline blanket over her, and closed her eyes.

Jameel sighed and tried to concentrate on the music coming through the earphones of his iPod. He thought perhaps once they arrived his grandfather would sit up and shake off the illness that had overtaken him, and that things would go on as always. He'd heard of miraculous recoveries. After the meal he reclined his leather seat and gave himself over to visions of Chloe crouched above her board, sailing from the top of a ramp with her arms spread like the wings of a beautiful bird, soaring to the beat of Audioslave, her golden hair aloft around her head in a perfect circle, like the rings of Saturn.

He awoke a few minutes later feeling as if he'd slept for hours. His father still stared straight ahead. He hadn't even loosened his tie. Jameel looked over at his mother, and caught her staring at him. "What?" Jameel mouthed, but his mother smiled softly and closed her eyes again.

Jameel pressed his forehead against the cool of the window beside him and was astonished to see the airplane was flying through a black velvet sky scattered with small, brilliant white lights that looked like stars. Larger white objects floated in and out of his vision—as one drifted closer, it looked like a person wrapped in a white sheet. Jameel leaned forward to get a better view.

The figure floated still nearer the aircraft with one hand extended. Jameel recognized his grandfather's twinkling eyes, full white beard, and highly arched black eyebrows. Their eyes locked, and his grandfather tilted his head to one side, sadness falling over his face like a veil. A chilly breeze blew through the aircraft and Jameel shivered. His grandfather slid back slightly and stretched his arm farther in Jameel's direction, but he slipped away from the aircraft. Jameel tried to reach out, but his hand bumped into the window. He leaned forward and watched until the figure grew smaller and then was indistinguishable from the stars.

Jameel turned to his father, who still sat staring straight ahead. "Daddy," he said quietly. His father turned to him. "I think Grandfather is gone." He shivered again, and his father drew a soft blue airline blanket around Jameel's shoulders.

"Why do you say that, Beta?" he asked gently.

"I saw him. He was outside . . ." Realizing how ludicrous he must sound, Jameel stopped mid-sentence.

"I think you've been dreaming," his father said. "Go back to sleep—we'll have a busy day when we get to Lahore. We'll be landing in a little more than an hour."

Jameel did go back to sleep, a fitful sleep, dreaming of skateboarding with Grandfather, while Chloe watched from a hospital bed. Grandfather leaned into his carves and Chloe, who was dressed in a white gown, clapped her hands and cheered.

15

Omar and Muti reached Number 5 Anwar Road in the darkest part of night. The door shutting behind them in the quiet of that hour sounded loud enough to awaken all of Gulberg.

They found Leyla pacing in a dressing gown in the front hallway. Omar turned to Muti.

"You'd better get some sleep," he said. "We have a lot to do tomorrow." Muti nodded and went up to her room.

She undressed slowly without turning on the light. She pulled on her pajamas, but tired as she was, she couldn't face the solitariness of trying to sleep. All she could think of was Baba in the hospital bed, a sheet pulled up over his face. Hadn't he been there in his body just moments before, the light lit behind his closed eyes, breathing in and out, his hand warm?

Muti sat in the small easy chair in the corner of the room, and clicked on the reading lamp beside it. She picked up a photo in a Persian frame inlaid with ivory and brass from the tabletop. The photo was of Baba—taken when he was about twenty years old, long before the responsibilities of being a tribal leader had weighed on him. Muti guessed it was a time when her grandfather, Baba's father, was the tribal leader. In the photo a polo mallet rested on his shoulder. He was tall and slim, his face clean-shaven and his hair dark. He looked very different, but his pointed eyebrows and mischievous grin were unmistakable.

As Muti looked at Baba's photo she heard voices from Omar and Leyla's room below hers on the ground floor. She listened to them talk through the water pipe that passed from their room up to hers and to the floor above. She heard the words they spoke, but something prevented her from putting them together and applying them to herself. She felt too numb to react to one more thing. Losing Jag. Finding her mother. Losing Baba. She couldn't absorb the loss or gain of one more thing.

Leyla's voice rose in anger, and suddenly the room felt chilly. Muti looked up—the window stood open. Warm air should have been pouring in through the screen. She heard the tree frogs outside. She thought perhaps she felt chilled because she was so tired.

Both voices downstairs were raised in angry disagreement. Mumtaz knew they were talking about her, but she could not admit the words into her consciousness. A Nepali shawl lay across the back of her chair, and she pulled it around her shoulders. The air grew colder still and a musty smell settled around her.

Muti lay down and pulled her sheet up over the Nepali shawl and thought of what Baba had told her and Jameel about the djinn. They were impish spirits, he'd said, sent by Allah to each person to teach something. Sometimes they were evident because of a change of air in the room. She couldn't think yet about the words from downstairs. She concentrated instead on what her djinni might be trying to tell her.

She thought of how she'd given away her mother's secret without even realizing it. She could trust Omar, she thought. But she did not like it that he knew her mother lived on the roof of the haveli. Once again the feeling of not belonging, of never being safe, rose up around her, and she didn't have the strength to fight it.

* * *

Downstairs Leyla continued pacing in the sitting room at the end of their bedroom. Omar had been telling her how Baba had died. "He actually looked peaceful," Omar said. "Perhaps because he knew things have been settled."

Leyla stared at the tops of the walls and then at the ceiling, all the while looking more anxious. "I haven't slept a wink," she said, her voice accusing, as if her exhaustion were Omar's fault.

"There are some other things I must tell you," Omar said. The tone of his voice rather than his words captured Leyla's attention. Omar was sounding more authoritative than he ever sounded.

"Jameel has been named tribal leader to succeed my father."

Leyla stared at him in disbelief. "Jameel!" she said. "Jameel!" Her words came out in a near shriek. "What about you? What about Jaffar?" She had put up with the old man's eccentricities, the slights, the honors bestowed on Baba by everyone from the sweeper to the Chief Minister of the Punjab Assembly, only because she knew that the cloak of leadership would pass from her father-in-law to her husband, and then to her son. That was how it should be!

"I refused the leadership long ago, when Uncle Rahim died," Omar said. "I've had enough of the intrigues of leadership. I watched Uncle Rahim get killed over power and I lost my stomach for it. I have no interest."

"But how long have you known?" Leyla asked. "Why didn't you tell me?"

"We had all been sworn to secrecy," Omar replied. "And the other thing is that Jameel and Mumtaz are to be married."

"Mumtaz?" asked Leyla as if she didn't understand what Omar had said. "How can that Gypsy possibly fit in—"

"Mumtaz is a bright girl. She is a direct descendant of my grandfather. She's a good girl, and she will be a good wife. She and Jameel are compatible, and it's settled, so there's no use making a fuss. This marriage will take place soon. We didn't want Nazir to get ideas in his head about upsetting the plans and taking control himself."

"And here I've been wasting my time trying to arrange

something in Okurabad," Leyla said accusingly. "You could have saved me the trouble—"

"It's time you got some sleep," Omar said, interrupting her. "I'm leaving now for the airport. We'll have a lot to do in the morning." His voice sounded as if it had squeezed through a very narrow opening in his throat. "At seven-thirty or so, Asrar can begin to telephone people from government. You call your family on your mobile, and I'll call my side of the family."

Leyla opened her mouth to say something, then shut it again. This was not the time to complain. She was not accustomed to her husband taking strong positions. She was not accustomed to his giving orders to the servants. She resumed her pacing.

I must take action, Leyla thought. She looked at her watch. In a few hours the muezzin would give the call for early morning prayer. She would not dither like Omar. She would take decisive action.

Leyla sat down at the desk in the front hallway and wrote out a note to Uncle Nazir telling him of Omar's plan for Baba's succession. If Omar wouldn't assume power, then Nazir should take over. That way Leyla would have time to put some plans in place for Jaffar's future as tribal leader. Nazir didn't have a son, and she had been careful to be kind to him when none of the rest of her father's wretched family gave him the time of day. When she had finished, she went to the cupboard under the stairway and fetched a light cotton chador, which she wrapped around herself as she walked briskly through the kitchen to the servants' quarters. She went straight to the door of Spin Gul's room and tapped lightly.

From behind the door she heard Spin Gul stirring. Leyla shared the driver with her mother, and his loyalty was split evenly between them. He had a highly developed sense of stealth. Leyla and Amina used him for errands they didn't want others to know about.

* * *

Muti lay in her bed and slowly absorbed the words she had overheard from downstairs. She was still too numb to react to the plans Baba and Omar and Jameel's parents had made for her and Jameel. She was used to feeling unsafe and unloved. She was used to not having a mother, to being all alone in the world except for Baba and Jameel. Suddenly she had a mother and the chance for a secure place in the family. But it felt strange and unreal, like a drama in which the actors read from a script that made little sense.

16

The flight arrived on time. Crowds of people looking for familiar faces among the travelers jostled under bright lights at the metal barricade outside the arrivals lounge. Asrar waved to catch Jameel's father's attention and made his way along the barricade to its end. Asrar touched his forehead and bowed deeply, then turned and extended his elbows to clear a path for them through the crowd to the VIP lounge. The night air was hot and heavy—much warmer than the daytime air of San Francisco. The noise of the crowd and traffic from Airport Road added to the feeling of heaviness. The din disappeared as if by magic as the door to the cool, quiet lounge swung shut behind them.

Jameel tried to imagine what Chloe would make of the effusive formality that greeted his family everywhere in Pakistan's Punjab province. Everyone knew them. His grandfather was a tribal leader, and Baba and Uncle Omar were members of the Provincial Assembly. Amirzai tribal lands spilled from Punjab westward almost to Baluchistan; he didn't even know how many thousands of hectares in all. Chloe's world was so different from his—she could never imagine how different, he thought.

He pictured her in all of the details that she'd described to him about her life: curled with her back against her mother in the double bed in the one-bedroom walk-up apartment on Turk Street; bumping into each other in the dark, narrow hallway outside the bathroom when she went to brush her teeth; sitting at a small, square table in a corner of the kitchen, drinking a glass of milk in one long chug. Some of the guys made fun of Chloe because she seemed to do nothing at all but skateboard. But she didn't care. She was better at it than any of them. Jameel's stomach ached at the thought of her.

Omar waited inside the airport's VIP lounge. He rushed forward and embraced Jameel's father and then Jameel, and held on to his sister Nargis's hand as they followed Asrar to a sofa with ornately carved wooden legs and love seats covered in silk to match the sofa. The furniture was arranged in a U at one side of the lounge. Asrar ordered tea for them, and hurried off to arrange for their luggage to be delivered to the car. Uncle Omar sat between his sister and Jameel's father and cleared his throat.

"Father died tonight," he began. He covered his mouth for a second with his fingertips, cleared his throat again, and went on. "He never regained consciousness. The ending was peaceful. Mumtaz, Selma, and I were with him." Tears welled along the rims of Omar's dark eyes, but he remained composed. Nargis lowered her face into her hands. Jameel's father and Uncle Omar both gave Jameel a long look, but otherwise his father did not react at all.

"He left this envelope in his desk for Jameel," Uncle Omar said, pulling a sealed parchment envelope from inside his vest and handing it to Jameel. Jameel turned the envelope over and saw his grandfather's hardly legible, loopy scrawl on the front: *For Jameel,* it said. It felt like a single sheet of paper. He held it as he imagined his grandfather had held it when he put it in the desk to be found after his death: lightly between his fingertips. He folded it carefully and slipped it into the back pocket of his jeans.

"Aren't you going to open it?" asked his father. Jameel shook his head. He couldn't imagine reading Baba's final words to him with his family watching. They were quiet for a moment before Omar spoke.

"We have many things to discuss," he said. They talked about details of the funeral, which would be before sundown that day. There was much to be done. His father and uncle seemed oddly restrained, Jameel thought. Perhaps it only seemed that way because Jameel felt so keenly that the world as he knew it had ended. It made him want to beat his fists on a wall and cry and scream.

Asrar returned and they followed him outside to where the car waited at the curb nearest the VIP lounge. Jameel felt as if his eyelids were made of sandpaper as he squinted against the bright overhead lights. The air was difficult to breathe, so damp, hot, and heavy that it seemed to part like a curtain before his face as he walked.

Two thin men in blue shalwar kameez, servants from Jameel's grandfather's house, stood with Khoda Baksh beside the thirty-year-old blue Mercedes Benz sedan with six suitcases and a metal trunk lashed to the rack on the roof. It was difficult to grasp that here were his grandfather's much-loved car, his driver and lifelong friend, and servants who had worked for the family their entire lives, but his grandfather was no more. When it comes right down to it, Jameel thought, life is just a flimsy veil, one that can be worn, then tossed aside with surprising ease. He thought of the image of his grandfather slipping past the airplane window to take his place among the stars.

The servants saluted them gravely as they stepped into the car. Khoda Baksh held the door as Jameel and his mother climbed into the back with Uncle Omar. Jameel's father sat in front. The air conditioner blew chilled air over them as the driver put the car into gear and pulled into the traffic heading for the airport exit. Dozens of flights arrived and departed from Lahore in the middle of the night, and the roads and parking lots were more crowded than they were at midday. Jameel craned his neck to look at the saluting servants until they were out of sight. He was vaguely aware of the jumble of cars, motor scooters, trucks, and buses that shrieked and rumbled around them, the green Provincial Assembly emblem on the front bumper alerting traffic that they had the right-of-way. Everyone in the car was silent.

When they reached the Gulberg area the headlights swept over the lovingly kept lawns and the tranquil canal overhung with willows that leaned to brush the water. Jameel began to feel the familiarity of the city where his father and uncles and grandfather had all lived when they were schoolboys, the streets where his mother and aunties walked to school every day when they were girls. Instead of the comfort he usually felt when he came here, he felt the cut of pain somewhere so deep inside him he couldn't identify exactly the place from which his grandfather had been excised.

As the car turned into Number 5 Anwar Road, Jameel felt a hand on his shoulder. He turned toward Uncle Omar, but his mother's brother stared straight ahead. Jameel looked down at his shoulder. No hand lay there, although he still felt its weight and warmth through his shirt.

They drove through the arched gateway, into the paved courtyard, and stopped before the red sandstone façade of his grandfather's house. Auntie Leyla came out through the front door just after the car pulled in and stood waiting under the tall, pointed arch of the main entry.

Jameel thought of the folded envelope tucked into the back pocket of his jeans. He felt it with his right hand, the same pocket that Chloe had hooked a finger into as she walked him to meet Javed a day earlier in his other world, his other time zone. He fought an urge to excuse himself right at that moment so he might go somewhere to open the envelope in private, and find out what his grandfather had to say before he died. Jameel felt a surge of anger at Baba for leaving so unexpectedly, before he'd had time to say goodbye.

He waited while the luggage was unloaded from the roof of the car and his parents made their salaams. Jameel had slept little on the plane, but he felt alert, on edge.

Jameel's parents had their own bedroom in his grandfather's house. Jameel slept in the room where his mother had slept as a girl. He wondered where other relatives traveling to Lahore for the funeral would sleep. Servants appeared from their quarters behind the house to haul the suitcases and trunk up the winding staircase in the front hall to the second floor.

Jameel greeted Leyla warmly and waited while his parents asked questions. He was too distracted by the stiff envelope in his back pocket to listen carefully. After waiting what seemed an acceptable time he excused himself to go to his room and read Baba's letter in private. He bounded through the brightly lit entry hall and up the stairs. The walls were painted with almond blossoms and fruit trees, and melons on vines twined down the corners of the room. The ceiling was even more ornately painted, and the plaster was embedded with bits of mirror that sparkled and reflected light from the huge lead-crystal chandelier that hung in the center of the hall. The chandelier was exactly like the one in the dining room. Jameel remembered when his grandmother had ordered the chandeliers from Venice. They arrived almost a year later in a crate that was taller than his Uncle Omar, loaded on a wagon pulled by four white oxen.

Upstairs Jameel gazed around his room, which also was ornately painted and mirrored, and thought again how blown away Chloe would be. He changed quickly into pajamas. He was relieved to be out of the collar of his shirt and the heaviness of jeans in the stifling heat and humidity of late monsoon season in Lahore. He took the envelope from his pocket and sat on the bed. Instead of tearing the envelope open, he smoothed it flat and retrieved a silver-handled letter opener from the desk in the corner of the room and slid it neatly under the flap, slitting the paper. He spread the letter from his grandfather flat and read it. It was dated three years earlier.

My Dear Jameel,

Now that I am gone, the first thing you must know is that beginning immediately you are my successor as leader of the Amirzai tribe. Your uncle and your parents and I decided the issue of succession long ago, almost immediately after your birth, and they will support you with their lives. We have kept this determination from you in order that you might live your life as normally as possible, unencumbered by the cares of leadership. I hope you will be finished with university before having to bear the weight of this responsibility. Other arrangements will be made shortly, and you will learn of them in due course.

Your Uncle Omar will hand over a ring containing the seal that has been the emblem of Amirzai leadership for hundreds of years. It is said to have been passed by the Holy Prophet Muhammad to our forefather Mahmet. Guard it carefully and use it wisely.

As leader of the Amirzai tribe you must act judiciously

to control all aspects of the lands, from the Lahore house to the farm at Okurabad, to the remotest small village of Amirzai tribesmen. Your Uncle Omar has full written guidelines, and he and your father will educate you as to your duties and responsibilities. You have traveled with me throughout Amirzai lands, and have seen how I go about doing things. I hope that also will guide you.

We have been blessed with peaceful times in the past. While patches of turmoil have disrupted life in parts of the country because of Islamist insurgents, our tribesmen have remained levelheaded. We have always treated them fairly and they have responded with loyalty.

Let Allah be your guide. Never lose sight of who you are and what you represent. Have courage and know I will be keeping watch.

Your loving grandfather,
Mahsood Jameel Muhammad Amirzai

Jameel's heart beat so hard his chest ached. He felt as if he'd been punched in the stomach. He couldn't quite comprehend all at once what his grandfather's letter meant. Certainly that his life in California was over. It meant that he and Chloe would never get to know each other well enough to see where their romance might lead them. Once he'd taken that huge first step of kissing her, life seemed filled with possibility. But now the future he'd imagined was impossible.

17

Shabanu greeted the monsoon sunrise standing beside the doorway of the pavilion watching another pigeon she'd released as it disappeared past the domes carrying another message for Ibne. The message asked him to meet her at the bus station in Bahawalpur and take her to her family in Cholistan. Dark clouds had fallen low over the Old City, and even in the dim light the domes of the Badshahi Mosque were luminous.

When she heard a footfall on the stone tiles that covered the roof, she expected to see Samiya with her breakfast. But something about the sound of the feet moving toward the doorway of her pavilion let her know it was not the familiar tread of either Selma or Samiya, and she stepped behind the painted wooden screen that separated her bed from the sitting area.

The carved, lacy panels that enclosed her living space had several magical qualities, one of which was that Shabanu could see out through the pavilion walls, while no one outside could see in. When she saw the tall, slender form of Omar, her mouth went dry and she felt faint.

"Shabanu?" he called softly, and she could not find her voice to answer. "Are you there?" She felt her feet were planted in the floor like the palm trees in the large Chinese wine pots in the courtyard downstairs. Omar was only a few feet away from the doorway to the pavilion when she moved out from behind the screen and he saw her.

"I'm sorry," he said, "I didn't mean to frighten you . . ."

"Come in, Omar," Shabanu said, hardly trusting her voice. "How did you know . . ."

"I overheard Mumtaz tell my father you were here, safe after all this time," he said. "Baba was unconscious. I don't think Mumtaz even knew she was telling him. She was trying to make him hear her, to let him know how grateful she was for his keeping her safe. Selma didn't want to let me come up, but I told her that I knew you were here." Shabanu said nothing, and Omar moved closer to her.

"Why?" he asked. "We were friends—why couldn't you let me know just that you were alive?" Shabanu studied him. His lips quivered and she could see a pulse beating in the side of his neck. Friends? she thought. And then she remembered that Omar couldn't know that she'd seen him wailing beside her graveside. He'd hardly changed at all—perhaps a few lines around his eyes, a few gray hairs—and he looked at her as he'd looked at her years before: as if he couldn't quite believe she was real.

"Because Nazir tried to force me to marry him after

Rahim died," she said after a moment. "He threatened to kill Mumtaz and me. Zabo and I escaped and Nazir shot at us. The bullet hit Zabo. I would gladly have died in her place."

"But why did you let me believe it was you?"

"It wasn't only you, Omar, it was you and Mumtaz and my entire family," she said gently. "Mumtaz would never be safe if all of you knew where I was. And you—you were about to marry Leyla and become heir to the tribal leadership . . ."

"And you thought it would be easier for me not to know you were alive?" His voice was strained, and tears stood at the rims of his eyes.

"I watched when you came to Zabo's grave," Shabanu said, "and by then it was too late!"

"I never told you how I felt," Omar said hoarsely.

"You were just like your Uncle Rahim," she said. "You would never have been able to live with yourself if you hadn't done what was expected of you. I used to resent Rahim's dedication to the family and the tribe—but I would never have respected him if he'd been any different. And you—you were the same."

"But I didn't live up to Uncle Rahim's honor!" he said miserably. "He died in my arms—the best man I ever knew—and then I thought you died for the same senseless reasons. Vendetta. Land. The family honor. It was enough of death—I didn't have the stomach for it. Perhaps I'd been in America for too long. When I told my father I couldn't be his heir as tribal leader I thought he'd never speak to me again. But he agreed. He and Nargis and Tariq and I met and decided that we could start all over again with Jameel."

"But Jameel is an American boy . . ."

"We need someone who can change the way people think," said Omar. "When I look into Jameel's eyes I can see that he's torn. He is very American in some ways. His view of honor is all Pakistani, but his sense of justice is American. He sees everyone's life to be of equal value to his. I hope the time is right to introduce that way of thinking here, and that he will be good for all of us."

"Haven't you had enough of manipulation—using people for political reasons? What if he doesn't want to lead the tribe? He's just a boy! What about his education?"

Omar's face colored. "What?" said Shabanu, sensing there was something else. He didn't answer immediately. He reached for her hand, but Shabanu pulled back. They were sitting on the Swati chairs facing each other.

"The details haven't been worked out," he said, "but I may as well tell you what else Baba's will says." Shabanu sat very still. "Shortly after the funeral, Jameel and Mumtaz are to marry. He's a fine young man. They will be good for each other." For a moment longer, Shabanu said nothing. "It was planned to give Mumtaz security as well as to bind the family together," Omar added.

"You can paint it however you choose," said Shabanu. "What about their education? What about letting them mature—giving them the chance to discover what they want for themselves?"

"We all thought Baba would live a long time," Omar said.

"Isn't this the kind of manipulation you and your father wanted to end with your modernization?" Shabanu asked.

"I must get back to Number 5," said Omar. "There's so much to do. The funeral will be late this afternoon—but I had to come to see you with my own eyes. May I come back?"

Shabanu shook her head. "I'm going to Cholistan, to my family," she said. Omar hesitated a moment. He looked as if he wanted to tell her things, and she wanted to tell him so many things that had grown in her heart over these many years.

"Will you come back?" he asked.

Shabanu nodded. "As long as Mumtaz is here I'll always come back."

18

Jameel got into bed. He closed his eyes, but immediately the words of Baba's letter played through his mind. He heard them in Baba's distinctively booming voice, as if his grandfather were reading the letter out loud.

When Baba's voice finally went silent the major fact of the letter and its profound impact on his life crowded out everything else: he would not return to his friends, to school, to Chloe, to his life. That was why his mother had packed all of his clothing. His first reaction was disbelief. Uncle Omar was Grandfather's only son—and should be next in line to rule the Amirzai people. And Jaffar should be next in the line of succession after his father. He turned on the light and read the letter again. What his grandfather wrote was clear and explicit—Jameel had not been mistaken about the letter's meaning.

His next reaction, mixed with the first, was anger. His parents and uncle, and especially his grandfather—the people he trusted most in the world—had known what was in store for him. They'd allowed him to believe he'd live a normal life—that he'd go to university and become an engineer, live in America, and follow his dreams. Without ever thinking about it, Jameel had taken this as a promise.

He stared at the letter in his hands and tried to harness some of the wild thoughts that swirled inside his head. Would his father and mother stay in Pakistan? Would they sell their house in California? Would Javed and Asma live with them here?

With shaking hands, Jameel stuffed the letter back into the envelope, put it into the drawer of the desk under the window, and got back into bed. But still he could not sleep. He wondered what other arrangements his grandfather referred to.

Jameel felt as if he didn't sleep at all in the next few hours, but he was awakened by a stripe of sunlight that had escaped from the edge of the window shade and fell across his eyes. He lay still for a moment, trying to reimagine his life here, as if his parents had never left Pakistan, as if he'd been born here and not in America, as if he'd expected to live here his entire life. But there was no recapturing what had never been.

A surge of angry energy propelled him from the bed. His eyes felt gritty from lack of sleep, but he was alert and tense. He pulled a shalwar kameez from his closet, dressed quickly, and fished out a pair of chappals, which he slipped his feet into, not bothering to pull the straps up and over his heels. Still tying the shalwar, he took the back stairs two at a time, the sandals slapping on the treads.

He heard voices from the dining room as he cut through the kitchen, where he snatched up a piece of paratha before pushing through the swinging door. His parents were seated at the highly polished table with Uncle Omar, Auntie Leyla, Mumtaz, and Jaffar. It seemed everyone was talking at once, and the talk stopped dead as he entered the room. He could tell Muti had been crying by the puffy redness of the skin around her eyes. She half stood when he came through the door, as if she wanted desperately to see him.

"Sit!" Auntie Leyla commanded, and Mumtaz sank silently back into her chair. He made his salaams hurriedly around the table, but everyone continued staring at him awkwardly. He didn't feel much like making small talk to ease things. The least they could do was feel uncomfortable, he thought.

He remembered the last time he'd arrived, at the beginning of the summer, when he and Muti and Jaffar all babbled happily at each other, catching everyone up on their news, the adults talking enthusiastically about plans for the summer. But then, everything was different this time, with Baba gone. Suddenly life was gravely serious.

Uncle Omar invited Jameel to sit, but he continued to stand, wolfing down the paratha. Muti nodded her head over one shoulder and spread one hand out on the table, all five fingers splayed before her. It was their signal to meet out in the garden in five minutes.

"May I be excused?" she mumbled, standing and leaving

before there was an answer. Uncle Omar was telling Jameel how various duties were to be divided up that morning in preparation for the funeral.

"You should come with me," he said. "People will be calling to pay their respects, and also to greet you as the new tribal leader." Jameel's eyes followed Muti's back as she walked through the French doors into the front hallway and out through the side door into the garden.

He waited, listening to Uncle Omar for a few more moments, and then excused himself. Conversation resumed around the table, and Jameel left through the French doors, the same way Muti had gone, ignoring his father's voice calling him back.

He hurried through the formal garden, past the swimming pool, and through the gate to the little arbor, where he found Muti sitting in the swing near the koi pond behind the rose trellis.

Muti was crying, the tears a wet film on her cheeks. He sat down beside her. She wiped at her face with the end of her dupatta, sniffing loudly. During the summer Auntie Leyla had commented several times that Muti could never quite overcome the "rough manners" she'd acquired from her mother's relatives. But Jameel knew the rough manners were a protest against Auntie Leyla and her treatment of Muti, who was proud of her mother's family.

"You've read Baba's letter?" she asked, sniffing one last time and rubbing at her nose with the heel of her hand. He nodded. They spoke softly so no one who might come into the garden would hear them.

"How long have you known?" he asked. His voice sounded unnaturally gruff. "Why didn't you tell me?"

"I only found out late last night, after Baba . . . after he died, after you were almost here. Believe me, Jameel, if I could have prevented you from coming in time, I would have done it. But that isn't all . . ." She reached forward and put her hand on his forearm. "Jameel, you and I are to be married—very soon! I heard Omar and Leyla—"

"To each other?" Jameel blurted. "Why me? Why shouldn't Uncle Omar lead the tribe? Why don't they leave me alone?"

"It's not just you!" said Muti, staring at him in disbelief. "What about me? They send me to school, encourage me to be educated, and then just . . . order me to marry you? Without any care for what I think? How do you think that makes me feel? I know you've got Chloe—but I have someone, too!" Jameel looked at her closely. They were silent for a moment. Jameel felt light-headed. The scent of jasmine floated through the garden.

"Look," Muti said, leaning forward again, whispering urgently, "I know the last thing you want is to marry me. But I don't want to marry you either—so don't act like I'm part of a plot to trap you!" She stopped speaking and her face crumpled. She hid behind her hands, and her shoulders shook as she cried. Jameel put his arm around his cousin's shoulders. He and Muti had always shared confidences. They'd comforted each other when Muti's puppy died of distemper. They'd told each other secrets all their lives. Marrying Muti would be like marrying his sister!

"Jameel," Muti said in a voice muffled by tears and her hands, "I love someone, too. Even if it's hopeless—I couldn't even think until now about what I heard Omar and Leyla say last night. I want to run away, go back to the desert . . ."

"They tricked us!" Jameel said, his voice quivering with rage. "If they'd told me, I would never have come, not even to see Grandfather!"

"That's exactly why they didn't tell either one of us," said Muti, wiping angrily at her tears and gulping away her sobs. Jameel was being so selfish—she wanted to tell him everything that weighed so heavily on her, and he was so absorbed in how he was affected—he wouldn't even hear her! Most of all she longed to tell him about her mother. And she knew she could not.

"How did you find out?" asked Jameel.

"The way I find everything out," she said. Jameel knew about the chair in the corner of her room and the sounds that traveled through the water pipe. "I came home from the hospital with Omar last night, and I heard them. They said the marriage would be arranged right after the funeral. That was early this morning, just a few hours after Baba died. They're afraid Uncle Nazir will try to make a grab for power."

Jameel stared at her. When he and Muti were children they cut their fingers and pressed them together, sharing their blood, like characters in old movies in America. Once she had saved him from a swarm of bees, beating at them with her dupatta and leading him to the swimming pool, jumping in with him and staying under the water until the bees flew away. They were cousins and they were best friends. But married?

"I'm sorry, Muti," Jameel said. "But my life—both of our lives—are just beginning. We have so much to look forward to . . ."

"And once we're married our lives will come to an end?" Muti looked at him hard. And then she smiled. "Maybe we should run away together . . . so we wouldn't have to get married!"

Jameel smiled slightly. "Yeah—that would be a twist! Why didn't you tell me that you've fallen in love? Who is it?" Muti lowered her eyes.

"Well," she said, sizing him up as if deciding whether to tell him, even now, "he's totally unsuitable. He couldn't be more wrong."

"He can't be more unsuitable than Chloe!"

"He's a Hindu," she said, and Jameel's eyes widened.

"Where'd you meet a Hindu boy?"

"At the Lahore Club. He teaches tennis there. His family is mixed—his father's family are Hindu. They fled Lahore during partition. He grew up partly here, with his mother's family, and partly in India, with his father. It's very complicated."

"Do they know?" he asked, inclining his head toward the house.

"You're joking! Auntie Leyla would kill me. Uncle Omar's heart would be broken. They'd never let me out of the house again." She paused. Her next thought had been that it would serve her mother right—and then immediately she felt ashamed. "We meet at the club, and sometimes Fariel and I go out and meet Jag at someone else's house." Muti looked back toward the house. "I have to go in," she said. "They've become more watchful than they were during the summer. And they'll be even more so now that you're here."

"How is this supposed to happen? When do they plan to tell us?"

Muti shrugged and rose to her feet. "Probably not until after the funeral. But then I should think they'd move quickly. Let's meet tonight—after the dinner, when they're saying goodbye to everyone in the front hall. I'll meet you here. Maybe we'll have some brilliant idea by then."

Jameel nodded. The thought of the responsibility of leadership and marriage and what he was giving up weighed so heavily on him that he had to concentrate to believe that these things would actually happen, unless . . . he didn't even know unless what. All he knew was that this new reality had begun to weigh on him like dirt heaped on a grave. Part of him wanted to run out the front door and keep going, without ever looking back. But where would he go? Another part of him was angry that his life had been so manipulated, without his ever having a choice or the chance to express an opinion. And still a third part of him said that he must do his duty, whether he liked it or not. Once again he had the overwhelming sense of being stuck between times and places.

19

Jameel came into the parlor to find his father and Uncle Omar looking for him. It was time for Baba's male relatives to bathe the body in preparation for the burial.

"But we have to talk about Baba's letter," Jameel said.

"There isn't time now," said his father gently, resting his hand on Jameel's shoulder and guiding him toward the stairway to the second floor, where Baba's body awaited preparation for burial. "After the funeral we'll have time to talk at length."

"But I don't want to do this!" Jameel said, stopping suddenly. Omar took Jameel's other arm and pulled him along gently.

"I promise we will spend as much time talking after the funeral as you need. Right now we have to get on with things here."

Jameel took a deep breath and followed his father and uncle into the master bedroom suite, where the body lay waiting on Baba's marriage bed. It might have been the only time his grandfather had waited patiently for anything, Jameel thought as they entered the room.

They worked quickly, with tenderness. Jameel washed his grandfather's hands, and felt the weight of the old man's immense bones covered with strands of muscle and paper-thin skin. Jameel's throat was so tight he could barely swallow, and his eyes ached with holding back tears. They were tears of anger as much as sadness. And also tears of guilt for feeling such strong anger on top of his sadness.

Inayatullah stood by and prayed as they worked. When they were finished they wrapped Baba in a seamless white shroud, which they tied at both ends. Jameel thought his grandfather looked like a sack of mail, and felt his tears rise again.

Jameel excused himself and went to his room to change into the silk shalwar kameez and vest laid out on his bed by his mother for the funeral. He blew his nose and wiped his eyes dry and looked into the mirror. He looked different—more mature—and he told himself it was his imagination.

Downstairs Auntie Selma came and wrapped her large, comforting arms around Mumtaz, resting her chin against the side of the girl's head.

"Your mother is leaving for Cholistan tonight," Selma murmured. "You should go with her." Muti pulled her head back and looked into Selma's eyes, which surprised her with their intensity, and wondered whether she knew of Baba's plans for her and Jameel. Perhaps she and Jameel should go to Cholistan with her mother. She nodded slowly.

* * *

The family spent the next hour and a half in the grand formal parlor, receiving guests who came to pay their respects. Muti sat with the women on one side of the room, its walls inscribed with verses from the Quran. Jameel was with the men on the opposite side of the parlor. Their grandfather's shrouded body lay upon a string cot with ornately cast silver legs in an open space at the front of the room. The whole time Inayatullah stood near the body, murmuring prayers, asking for forgiveness for Baba's soul.

Jameel's mind clicked over like one of his grandfather's beloved engines. He considered ways out: it would be difficult. His mother and father kept all of their passports and traveler's checks in the vault in Baba's study, and he didn't know the combination. He only had a little money, the fifty rupees on his dresser and the few U.S. dollars he'd had in his jeans pocket when he left for the airport. And he doubted he could change that to rupees—certainly not without his passport.

The governor of Punjab Province was first to pay his respects, dressed in a Western suit and moving down the first row of seats where Jameel's father, Uncle Omar, and he stood to shake the governor's hand. Three long-stemmed fans swirled overhead.

The governor was followed by many dignitaries from the Punjab Provincial Assembly, and then by tribal leaders from all over Pakistan, followed by doctors, lawyers, businessmen, ambassadors, consuls general, and other prominent Lahoris. Last came the farmers of the Amirzai tribal lands, mourners—many of whom had taken buses and then walked the rest of the day, some in bare feet, to get there—in a line that snaked around the garden, through the front gate, and out into the street.

As Jameel sat with his family he felt several times the light warmth of a hand on his shoulder. It was the same hand, he thought, that had touched him in the car on the way from the airport; Jameel sensed it was his grandfather, letting him know he was near. Each time Jameel turned to see, nobody was there.

Once Jameel caught the eye of Uncle Nazir, and when he did, Nazir continued staring at him. Jameel realized Uncle Nazir had done the same thing as they bathed Grandfather's body. Jameel stared back this time, and eventually Nazir looked away. With all of the greetings and condolences and handshakes and bear hugs, Jameel didn't have time to think much more about his misfit uncle.

Late in the afternoon the procession, led by Maulvi Inayatullah, formed to accompany the body to the burial ground near the gate of the Badshahi Mosque, not far from the tomb of Alama Muhammad Iqbal, Pakistan's national hero and poet. The hand on Jameel's shoulder was a light and constant touch, and Jameel had grown so used to it that he hardly noticed it was there.

As the procession neared Badshahi Mosque they passed a knot of Amirzai village women who keened and beat their chests with their fists. Jameel winced at this display of grief, but he knew it was traditional, and he passed by the women without speaking or looking at them.

The rest of the funeral was a blur of faces and hands shaking his hand, dry-eyed mourning, the maulvi's prayers, the family murmuring the Janazah, asking for forgiveness to speed Baba on to the next world. Over everything lay the sense that an era had passed.

In keeping with the old man's wishes, a festive dinner followed under a red, green, and blue shamiana in the garden at Anwar Road, with men and women served together from one common table, just as Baba always insisted. The women filled their plates, and then, out of habit, stood on one side of the garden under the shamiana. The men retreated to the other side. Because no curtain was raised between the two parties, Jameel caught Muti's eye several times. Each time he looked at her she was watching him.

As the guests began to leave, Jameel was overcome by jet lag. He nearly fell asleep on his feet.

"Go to bed, Beta," his mother said. "Tomorrow is another day." She laid her palm against his cheek and smiled at him tenderly. Jameel felt the hand that had been on his shoulder drawing him now by the elbow in the direction of the garden. For the first time the hand was insistent, rather than gentle, and he had to fight against it to move in the general direction of the front hall so his mother and father would see him heading up to bed instead of to the garden to meet Muti. The hand pulled steadily at his elbow, causing him to walk in a wobbly diagonal line between the hallway that would lead to the back garden and the arch to the main stairway. To end the struggle, Jameel came to a stop.

"Stop pulling at me," he said under his breath to the spirit that commanded the hand. "You'll land me in trouble." He was standing under the marble arch in the entry to the main hall when he caught a glimpse of movement overhead and heard a sharp screech of metal. He looked up to see the crystal chandelier, one of the two his grandmother had ordered from Venice, tilt crazily to one side. Another screech, and the cables holding it parted and the whole thing, which stood as high as a man and weighed about a thousand pounds, crashed to the marble floor, accompanied by a shower of sparks as bare wires danced about under the ceiling.

The deafening crash was followed by the absurdly delicate tinkling of crystal drops and beads falling down through the structure of the chandelier onto the marble floor. It was as if the entire room were caught in a still photo. Then a chaotic chorus of women screaming, men shouting, and running footsteps burst the silence. Miraculously, no one had been in the front hall when the chandelier fell.

Jameel realized with a shudder that he might have been under the chandelier when it fell if it hadn't been for the insistent hand on his elbow. The touch was gone now, and Jameel took advantage of the confusion to run to the back of the hallway and through the French doors that led out to the garden. There, in the hidden arbor as before, he found Muti sitting on the swing. Someone had lit lanterns, which glinted on the little pool. Small rings appeared on the glassy surface of the water, where his grandfather's iridescent koi fed on mosquitoes.

"Did you see—" he began, but Muti was already nodding her head vigorously.

"I felt someone's hand on the small of my back, pushing me out the door," she said. "My feet could barely keep up. I heard the crash, but I couldn't turn back."

"The same thing happened to me—someone was dragging me by the elbow—but nobody was there!" Jameel said. "What do you think . . ." Muti shook her head impatiently.

"I've been thinking about a way to get out of here," said Muti. She looked determined. Jameel sat next to her on the swing.

"Where would we go?" he asked.

"I don't have time to tell you right now. Do you have any money?" Jameel shook his head.

"How much do we need?" Jameel asked. "Who'd help us without our telling them what we're doing?" Muti bit her lips. How could she tell Jameel about her mother? She took a deep breath and stood abruptly.

"We need enough for a taxi and bus tickets to Bahawalpur," she said.

"I only have about fifty rupees," he said. "It's upstairs."

"That's about what I have—it isn't enough."

"Why Bahawalpur?" asked Jameel.

"We don't have time," Muti said. "I'm going to call . . . someone on my mobile phone," she said. "I know where we can go—someone who will help us."

"Who are you calling?" Jameel asked. "Fariel? You know her family will have to call Omar. Nobody's going to help us!" Muti held up her hand for him to be quiet and dialed Selma's number. It rang several times. She was about to flip the phone shut when she heard Samiya's voice.

"It's Mumtaz," she said into the phone. "May I speak . . ." She couldn't bring herself to ask for her mother, but Samiya hesitated only a second before understanding.

"I'll take the telephone to her," said Samiya. "It'll be a few minutes. Hold on."

"Hurry!" Mumtaz breathed into the phone.

20

Jameel felt sick. He knew they would have to move quickly. He trusted Muti, but he didn't like not knowing where they were going. He swallowed hard. He had never done anything so disobedient before. His parents hadn't exactly told him not to go anywhere, but he knew that they trusted him, and he hated to break their trust, even now when they had broken their trust with him. But in the morning everything would be different. He would officially be the Amirzai tribal leader, his betrothal to Muti would be announced, and it would be too late to get away. He rose to his feet. The exhaustion that had nearly paralyzed him earlier was gone. He felt the blood rushing through his veins, and the vibration of the traffic two blocks away. It was as if the exhaustion and the crashing chandelier and the need to get away had heightened his awareness.

Jameel walked to the small gate in the garden wall to keep watch while Muti talked on the telephone. He looked across the large formal garden behind the house, which was perfectly symmetrical in its arrangement of rose beds and rows of fountains and perennial beds. Baba had laid it out years ago in a pattern similar to that of the Shalimar Gardens. Every day the mali took the dead blooms from the plants. He and his helpers spread out in a line, squatted, and trimmed the grass to velvet perfection with steel scissors.

Jameel thought about what he and Muti were doing. There was no escape from tradition and duty to family. He knew the price many people paid for trying to get out of what was expected of them. He'd heard stories of young people trying to run away because they were in love. Their families hunted them down, sometimes killed them. He shuddered. He didn't think his family would do that, but Jameel knew his father would never rest until he was found. And he was sure Uncle Omar would never rest until Muti was safe.

They couldn't get to their passports and credit cards. And then it dawned on him: Muti planned to go to her mother's family in Cholistan.

As he thought these things a bright light appeared at the head of the big garden. It was so bright he couldn't see anyone behind it. The light looked as if it bobbed along on its own. A sharp intake of breath at his shoulder made him turn toward Muti, who had come up behind him. As he turned, a bolt of flame shot past his head, missing him by centimeters. If he'd been still it would have hit him in the face.

In the split second it had taken the djinni to soar through the garden they saw a ghostly figure in a pale shalwar kameez scurry away from the fence near where they had been sitting a few seconds earlier. They could see the tiny beads embroidered in a Pashtun-style skullcap twinkling in the lights from the swimming pool.

"It's Spin Gul," said Mumtaz. She had never liked Leyla's driver, who narrowed his eyes insolently when he looked at her, rather than respectfully look away as the other servants did. "He was listening to us!" She grabbed Jameel's hand and pulled him back toward the koi pool.

"Wait!" said Jameel. "We'll be trapped in here." Muti continued to pull at his hand.

"No—we can get out! Come this way," she said, her breath shaking. She still clutched her mobile phone to her ear. Jameel leaped across the koi pool, but Muti didn't quite make it. She recovered her balance, knee-deep in water, and extended her hand for Jameel to pull her out. She shook her cell phone, but it didn't appear to have gotten wet.

"Come," she said, and he followed her to the brick wall at the edge of the garden. The wall was lined with lime trees, and Muti grabbed one of the lanterns beside the wall where they'd sat. She held it high, looking for something behind the lime trees.

"Hurry!" he said. He looked over his shoulder and saw the djinni grow brighter as it approached again from a different direction. Muti thrust the lantern into his hand and pulled on the branch of a lime tree at the base of the wall. Behind the tree a gate opened, and Muti crouched to crawl through. Jameel followed, bringing the lantern with him and letting go of the lime tree branch at the last second.

Muti sank down on the other side with her back against the wall, sucking at a vicious scratch on her arm.

"Thorns," she muttered, rising to her feet. "Let's go."

"Did your call get through?" Jameel asked. "Did you find a place where we can go at this hour?"

"The phone went dead," she said. "I've been redialing. The battery has a good charge and the signal is strong here, but there's a strange howling sound in the phone. It was the djinni! I've *never* had that happen before."

"Why?" he asked. "I thought the djinn were supposed to help us!"

"They did!" said Muti. "If it hadn't been for that light we never would have known Spin Gul was spying on us. Come—we'll just go there . . . I know she'll help."

"Who? Fariel?" he asked, but Muti was already running down the lane that passed along the back garden wall.

They left the lantern outside the gate in the hope of confusing the djinni—or anyone who might be following—and ran along the bank of the canal to an intersection where traffic rushed past in either direction. Jameel looked back down the alley they'd just left while Muti watched for a break in the traffic. The light, which clearly was disembodied, bobbed around the lantern outside the small gate, as if confused momentarily by the motionless light.

Muti grabbed Jameel by the hand and pulled him across the street, with motor rickshaws bleating, cars honking, and brakes squealing around them. A bus overflowing with men clinging to the roof and sides screeched as it swerved to miss them. On the other side of Anwar Road, Muti ran down another alley and out onto the busy thoroughfare called Makhdoom Sahib Road. She flagged down a motor rickshaw and they both climbed inside.

"We have to stop at Fariel's to get some money," Muti said. "We can ask the rickshaw-wallah to wait while I go inside."

It was a short ride to Mustafa Road at the edge of the Cantonment area. Muti instructed the rickshaw-wallah to wait at the end of the lane that ran behind the back wall of the compound. The man grumbled, but they left him to himself, knowing he'd wait rather than not be paid.

They held hands and ran together down the dark lane until they came to a gate guarded by a sleeping chowkidar. Quietly, without waking the old guard, Muti slid the bolt from the latch and let them both into a small garden planted with vegetables.

Lights from the house reflected from the round shapes in neatly planted rows of eggplants, squash, and tomatoes. They followed the planted rows until they reached the broad veranda that spanned the back of the house. Muti found the third window to the right of the back door. The bottom half of the window was screened, and Muti tapped lightly on the glass above: two taps, a pause, and three taps.

They heard the rustle of bedclothes and Fariel's sleepy voice at the window. "Who is it?" she whispered. When she saw it was Muti, she said, "What are you doing out at this hour after your grandfather's funeral?"

Muti shushed her and told her she needed some money. Fariel unlatched the window screen and opened it enough for Muti to come inside. "Do you mind waiting here?" she asked, turning to Jameel.

"Who's with you?" Fariel whispered.

"My cousin Jameel," said Muti. She heard Fariel exhale.

"Oh, bring him in," Fariel said. In the dim light from the garden Muti could see Fariel wrapping a white chenille robe around herself. Jameel stood next to where Muti was just climbing through the window. He'd never been in a girl's bedroom. If his parents found out, they'd disown him!

"You want to stand out there and get caught?" said Fariel. "You'd better come inside." She held the screen while he heaved himself over the windowsill and landed on the floor inside. Fariel pulled the window shade closed and lit a small reading light on the wall over the bed.

Fariel was small, with wrists so tiny Jameel had an urge to circle them with his thumb and forefinger. Her eyes were enormous, with cinnamon-colored irises. Her thick black hair was so short it stood up on her head, making her look like a small boy. She couldn't be more different from his cousin, he thought. Muti was tall and slender, with graceful hands and arms. Her movements were languid, and this evening she wore her hair in a braid that hung down her back. Fariel spoke and moved like a hummingbird darting among flowers.

"What are you doing out at this hour?" Fariel asked, sleep in her voice, but not in her alert eyes. Muti explained quickly that they were running away. Fariel knew about Leyla's mistreatment. Her eyes widened as Muti explained.

"I don't have time to tell you the whole story," she said.

"We need some money. We have a rickshaw waiting at the end of the lane." Fariel looked at them both and raised her eyebrows.

"Let me see if I have this right," she said with a hint of sarcasm in her voice. "You're running away together so you don't have to marry?"

"Come on, Muti," said Jameel. "If she won't help us, there's no sense wasting time."

"Did I say I wouldn't help?" said Fariel. "I just don't understand. Where are you going?"

"I can't tell," said Muti quickly. "And it's better for you not to know. I'm sure Omar will be here looking for me before long, and you'll be able to say honestly that you don't know where we've gone. Just tell the truth."

Fariel nodded. Jameel and Muti sat on one of two beds in Fariel's room, and Fariel sat on the other bed, facing them.

"So—how much do you need?" asked Fariel.

"Enough to leave Lahore," said Muti. "We don't have credit cards, so it'll have to be enough for two bus fares."

"I have about two hundred rupees," Fariel said, "but you'll have to wait here while I go into the front hall to get it."

"Hurry!" said Muti. "Omar will be here soon looking for us!" At almost the same time they heard a noise from the garden near the window they'd just climbed through. And a second later there was banging from somewhere in the house.

"The front door!" said Fariel. She doused the reading light and whispered, "Here, take this." She swept a small pile of notes from the top of her dresser and shoved them into Muti's hand. "It should be about a hundred rupees." She leaned out the window and whispered, "Who's there?" No one answered and she saw no one.

"Follow me," she whispered, gesturing toward the hallway. She led them to a door that opened onto a side yard, where the compound wall was close to the house. "Go through that gate," she said. "The lane will take you back the way you came in." Muti gave her a quick hug, and she and Jameel ran down the lane to the alley, where they heard the putt-putt of the waiting rickshaw.

21

They directed the rickshaw-wallah to drive to the old walled city, looking over their shoulders to see whether anyone had come out through Fariel's back gate, looking for them. But the alley remained dark and empty—no disembodied lights, no angry relatives.

"You might as well tell me where we're going," said Jameel, sitting back on the hard bench seat as the rickshaw putted down the lane toward Muallam Road. Muti shifted her eyes from the road behind them, slower to relax than her cousin. She looked at Jameel but said nothing. "I'm going to know soon enough anyway!" Muti gazed out at the buses and automobiles that careened around them as they swerved out into the main thoroughfare.

"We're—we're going to my mother," she said finally.

"Stop talking in riddles," Jameel said irritably. As they approached Mustafa Road, the press and din of traffic intensified and the smell of exhaust seeped around the edges of the plastic side curtains.

"I'm not," said Muti. "I'm serious." She had to shout above the blaring horns to explain how her mother had sent for her and why she'd hidden for such a long time. When she finished, Jameel rubbed his hand over his mouth and then dropped it to cover Muti's hand on the seat between them.

"How long have you known that Uncle Nazir killed your father?" he asked. Muti shook her head.

"I didn't know until my mother told me. But I've never felt safe around my father's family—I don't trust any of them, except for Baba, Auntie Selma, and Omar. And you. I've always tried to put it out of my mind. The other night after Baba died, I remembered something for the first time since it happened, around the same time that my mother disappeared.

"Do you remember that little fawn I had? Choti was her name." Jameel nodded, and she told him about the fawn's death.

"Did Uncle Nazir have something to do with Choti's disappearance?" Jameel asked.

"I don't know—Uncle Nazir was hunting with my father that day," she said. "My father would never have killed my pet. He gave her to me. It was just another reminder of how little control my mother and I had over our lives. After my mother told me Uncle Nazir had killed my father, I felt certain somehow he'd killed Choti." She shivered, although the moist heat of the evening pressed around them.

"I caught him staring at me during the funeral, and when we were preparing Baba's body for burial," said Jameel. "He's always been creepy—how is it that we never noticed before?" Muti shrugged and they were silent for a time.

"There have been so many uncomfortable things in my life I hardly noticed him," Muti said.

"I'm so dense," Jameel said. "I never realized until the dinner just before we went back to San Francisco how bad things were for you living with Leyla. I've been such a self-centered—"

"Don't worry," Muti said. "I looked forward to seeing you every summer, and you were always my friend. We both have our reasons for not wanting to marry each other—but your friendship has been so important to me!" Jameel smiled, and suddenly felt disconcerted. He changed the subject.

"Does Uncle Omar know about your mother?" Jameel asked, and Muti nodded. "Once he realizes we're not at Fariel's, won't he look for us next at the haveli?"

"He's probably on his way there now," she said. "I'll try telephoning my mother again to see if she'll meet us at the bus terminal. My mother is going to see her family in Cholistan. Auntie Selma said it was important for me to go with her—perhaps because Omar has told her about the plans for us to be married. All I know is that my mother is going tonight. Let me just try calling her again."

Muti punched in Auntie Selma's number. This time Samiya picked up the phone immediately. "Are you okay?" she asked. "Your mother is right here."

Shabanu's voice was calm and deliberate when she spoke into the telephone.

"Don't come to the haveli," her mother said. "I'm sure they will come looking for you. I've telephoned Ibne at Okurabad to meet us and take us to Grandmother and Auntie Sharma in Cholistan. Where are you?" Muti said they were about fifteen minutes away.

"Meet me outside Akbari Gate," said Shabanu. "Since they're coming by car they'll come the other way." Muti asked if her mother had clothes she might bring for Jameel and two burqas.

"Your father's clothes are still here," Shabanu said. "I'll find something for him."

"Uma," said Muti, "is it safe for you to be out? Jameel and I are both worried about Uncle Nazir." It was the first time she'd used her childhood name for her mother, and it didn't even sound strange to her.

"It's dangerous, but we'll be careful. Hurry—we won't really be safe until we reach Cholistan."

When she'd flipped the telephone shut, Muti leaned forward and ordered the rickshaw-wallah to take them to Akbari Gate. She sat back in the seat. Now that they had a plan, Muti could almost relax as the rickshaw weaved its way among other motor rickshaws and brightly painted trucks and automobiles and buses.

Outside the Akbari Gate a woman in a gray burqa paced back and forth in front of a bulging woven satchel that sat on the ground behind her. The red sandstone archway rose into a graceful domelike structure above and behind her, and

Mumtaz wondered how many similar dramas had taken place with people entering and leaving the Old City through these gates over the centuries. The burqa flared out around her mother's legs when she reached the curb and turned abruptly to pace back in the opposite direction.

When Shabanu saw the motor rickshaw, she picked up the bag and ran with it banging against her legs to the opposite corner. The rickshaw pushed across the traffic to the curb and lurched to a stop.

Shabanu put the carpet bag in the front beside the driver and pulled from it a burqa that she handed to Mumtaz. She squeezed into the backseat, with Mumtaz between her and Jameel.

"Uma," said Muti, "this is Jameel." Shabanu pulled the side curtains shut around them and pushed the burqa back from her face to study him.

"You were five years old when I last saw you, Jameel," Shabanu said, laying her palm gently against his cheek. "You've grown to look like your Uncle Omar." Jameel smiled and ducked his head. He was pleased that he looked like his uncle.

"Uma," said Muti, "the other burqa is for Jameel." Jameel's eyes widened.

"It's one thing for you to wear one," he said, and Muti took the burqa from her mother, thrusting it into his hands.

"Anyone looking for us will be watching for a boy and a girl," she said, "not three women." Jameel stared at her for a moment, sighed, and pulled the burqa over his head as Muti put hers on.

"We must get away as quickly as possible," said Shabanu, pulling her own burqa back into place. "I left the haveli by the back gate, and as I came around the corner a man in a white shalwar kameez and a mirrored skullcap was coming down the lane toward the front gate. Something about the way he watched over his shoulder made me distrust him."

Muti and Jameel exchanged glances.

"Spin Gul, Leyla's driver," said Jameel.

"The most logical thing would be for us to take the bus directly to Bahawalpur. And so I think we should take the train to Multan instead, and Ibne will meet us there. I asked Samiya to telephone him and let him know after I was gone. He'll take us to my family near Bijnot. I haven't let them know we're coming, but Ibne knows where they are."

"Has anyone telephoned from Number 5 Anwar Road?" asked Muti.

"Auntie Selma telephoned to tell me about the hullabaloo after the chandelier fell. She said that you and Jameel had gone missing, and that I should keep an eye out for you," said Shabanu, and then she added, "I know about the wedding plans. We'll talk about it later, when we've reached the desert."

The rickshaw slowed as they neared the stationary crush of traffic near the train station. Shabanu told the driver to stop, leaning forward to thrust a twenty-rupee note into his hand. Jameel took the satchel, and the three of them got out into the road and made their way to the train station on foot.

22

Jameel and Muti waited on a bench while Shabanu purchased their tickets for places in the train's third-class section. Despite their being hidden under burqas, Muti watched anxiously for anyone she might recognize. Omar and Nargis might think to look for them at the train station when they weren't at the bus depot. But if they did, it was most likely they would look on the platform for first-class travelers. And Uncle Nazir would look there for them as well.

Shabanu came back with their tickets. They had about an hour to wait until the train was to leave. They made their way to the third-class platform for the Multan train and sat down on a bench. Other passengers spread cloths and sat on the concrete platform. Many others milled about. Muti looked at the people waiting in clusters, eating from hampers, so many people it seemed impossible that all of them could fit on one train.

Jameel went off to find a chai-wallah to get them some tea and something to eat. Despite his wearing the burqa, Muti worried that he looked masculine. His walk was too square and vigorous.

She decided to put her concerns out of her mind. The crush of good-humored travelers, the burqas, and being with her mother made Muti feel safe. The feeling of safety—perhaps for the first time in ten years—filled Muti's heart and she began to weep silently. The well of her tears seemed bottomless. Without speaking, her mother took Muti into her arms, settling back against a pillar, and cradled her like a small child. Muti held on to her mother as if she were a life raft.

Jameel found them that way, and after a while Muti sat up and wiped her face with the flats of her hands. The three of them ate curry biscuits and drank sweetened red tea with buffalo milk, and waited for the train.

When they were seated on the wooden slat benches in the third-class coach, the satchel tucked behind their legs, they were happy to be under way. Exhausted by the events of the previous days filled with death and other partings, they slept fitfully, rocking to the rhythm of the train. The third-class compartment was so jammed with people and bedrolls and satchels, even some baby goats being taken as gifts to relatives in the country, that there was no danger of falling off the bench.

It was late at night when the train pulled into Multan, slowing as it approached the outskirts. The city was strangely quiet, lit only at major intersections. The air was clear from the day's rain, and the mud still oozed in the streets.

They got down from the train holding tightly to each other's hands. Jameel carried the large satchel, and they fought their way against the waves of people toward the first-class platform, where Ibne would be waiting to meet them. Shabanu and Mumtaz pushed their burqas away from their faces so they could better see where they were going.

When Shabanu saw Ibne in the crisply pleated, sharp white turban and the black velvet vest inset with bits of mirror glinting in the light from the streetlamps, it was just as she'd seen him the first time seventeen years before, and her heart filled with gratitude to her husband's most loyal servant. Shabanu remembered herself from the first time, too, a small desi girl in bare feet destined for marriage to a much older, wealthy man from a family filled with intrigues.

Ibne bowed to Shabanu, and she nodded in return, and lowered her eyes.

"How good to see you, memsahib," he said. Shabanu smiled.

"And it's wonderful to see you, Ibne," she replied, her voice choked with the memory of all that time ago.

Ibne led them to the car, Rahim's old sedan in perfect condition as if Ibne had just delivered him to the Provincial Assembly in it. Ibne put the satchel in the trunk, and they all piled in, Jameel in front with Ibne, and Shabanu and Mumtaz in the back.

They were quiet as Ibne concentrated on threading the car

among sleepy passengers fresh from the train, many of them balancing bundles of clothing and bedrolls on their heads. When they came to the edge of the city the car picked up speed.

"Your father and mother know we're coming," said Ibne. "They were so joyful to learn both of you would be with them again. Your Auntie Sharma and her daughter Fatima are there—all waiting for you in Bijnot."

Before getting into the car, Jameel had pulled the burqa off over his head. He sat slumped into the corner of the front seat by the passenger door. He watched the scrub of the desert thin outside the windshield as the car hurtled through the night. A line of pale greenish light was appearing on the horizon, a precursor to the monsoon sun, and he wondered what the next day would bring.

He thought of Mumtaz, who sat quietly in the backseat while Ibne and Shabanu talked of the people in Rahim's household, those who still lived at the farm in Okurabad. No one from Rahim's family had lived in the house since his death. Ibne had run the farm with occasional visits from Omar and Baba. Jameel had been to Rahim's farm with Baba and Omar so many times, never once guessing that he would be the proprietor one day. As he faced every new situation, the altered reality of his life jolted him all over again. If Jameel were to become tribal leader, he would decide when to plant the sorghum, and how to deal with problems of the tribesmen who lived nearby, what cattle to put on the land, when to divert the irrigation channels, and what other crops to grow. The locusts would be his problem. And the hill torrents, and feuds, and diseases of cattle and tribesmen.

He had been so self-absorbed he hadn't been thinking of Mumtaz—it was as if Baba's death and the djinni and the sad separation from his former life had happened only to him. Not only had Mumtaz lost Jag and Baba, but she was adjusting to having her mother back and to the idea of marrying him—and he'd made it so clear he wanted to escape. Jameel looked into the rearview mirror at his cousin. She had pushed the burqa back, and he could see one side of her face as she stared out the window. She looked as if she was in shock. But perhaps it was just the greenish lights from the dashboard that lit her profile dimly.

Suddenly Ibne's foot slammed down on the brake, and Jameel jerked his head around in time to see in the headlights a huge U-shaped barrier made of rocks that crossed the road just where it straightened after a curve around a hill. The rock barrier prevented them from turning to either side. Ibne struggled to control the car, but it swerved violently and spun in what seemed like slow motion, slamming sideways into the boulders. Jameel was aware of his body being hurtled against the dashboard, his head cracking against the post between the dash and the side door, things flying past, and then a black nothingness.

* * *

Mumtaz awoke with one side of her face in the dirt. She had been thrown from the car. Her body felt broken, and her mouth was filled with blood. She wanted desperately to sit up, to see whether her arms and legs worked, whether her mother was okay, and Jameel. But she heard men's voices, and from somewhere in her head came the warning to stay still and quiet in the dirt.

She managed to open her eyes slightly, and through her eyelashes she saw men milling about. Her mother, still covered in her burqa, sat beside her. She saw Jameel kneeling on the ground. Masha' Allah, God's will, he looked dazed but not seriously hurt. A large man stood between Mumtaz and Jameel, his back to her. Muti's blood went cold as she recognized the tailored tan silk waistcoat that Uncle Nazir had worn what seemed years ago at Baba's funeral.

She opened her eyes a little more and she saw other men with rifles, all facing Jameel. And she remembered someone—was it Omar?—saying that Nazir might try to take over the tribal leadership. And she remembered Auntie Selma saying Nazir was a toothless tiger, and her mother saying you must never trust a tiger, even a toothless tiger.

As Mumtaz's head cleared, she saw her father's car, twisted metal lying on its side, with smoke rising from the place where its engine should be. She recognized it only by the pale blue color of the parts that weren't twisted and burned beyond color and shape. One wheel was revolving slowly, like a fan on a sultry day. And the green Punjab Provincial Assembly emblem still sat proudly on an absurdly shiny bumper.

Slowly the likely consequences of what had just happened began to dawn on her: that in his grab for power Nazir would likely shoot each of them, one by one. But she never had time to finish the progression of thought through the murk of pain in her head.

Suddenly there was loud noise all around. And scuffling, and running, and men grunting. She saw Omar, still dressed in the fine silk shalwar kameez that he had worn for the funeral, raising a rifle to his shoulder and taking careful aim, and the recoil of the rifle butt against his shoulder as Nazir seemed to fly up into the air feet first, and then crash to the ground in a crumpled pile.

Mumtaz closed her eyes, and when she awoke again, there was a sharp sting in her nostrils and she gagged on something strong, and her eyes teared, and she could only see white all around her.

23

The sounds were ordinary sounds, a clink of metal and water pouring, Auntie Selma's deep, gravelly voice, the click and whir of a fan overhead. Someone was washing her face. She struggled against the hand that held the vial of smelling salts, and someone said, "She's awake!"

Sitting before her was Auntie Selma, and at her shoulder was her mother, and beside her mother was Jameel. They were all dressed in white. Of course, she thought: Baba's funeral. Her mother's arm was in a sling. Jameel had a bandage wrapped around his head. Her first thought had been "Where's Baba?"

"Where am I?" she asked, and their faces whirled slowly once or twice before coming into focus. Her mouth hurt and her words sounded fuzzy. She felt as if a large piece of wood wrapped in cotton wool pressed down on her tongue.

"You're fine, darling," said Auntie Selma. "You bit your tongue—nearly bit it off!" Arms were helping her to sit. "You're in my bed in the haveli. The doctor said tongues heal quickly, and you will be fine."

Her next thought made her stomach lurch: They were going to make her marry Jameel. And he didn't want her. She looked up at Jameel and his brow was creased. He swiped a hand across his eyes, which were glistening with tears. She must look a mess, she thought. She reached up and touched her mouth. Her teeth seemed to be intact.

"How long have I been here?" It might have been days, she thought. Her words came out sounding like "Nowon haha knee?"

"Since this morning," said her mother. Auntie Selma stood then and offered Shabanu her chair.

"Uma!" said Mumtaz, and tears filled her eyes.

"Don't worry, little one," her mother said, stroking her face. "You're safe. You're going to be fine."

"Wha hahenned?"

They told her how Spin Gul had followed them to the train station and telephoned Nazir, who flew his airplane to Multan to get there before the train arrived. He'd ordered workers from his farm to build the stone barrier across the road, and after the crash he was about to shoot Jameel when Omar and Jameel's father appeared. Omar had shot and killed Nazir. Jameel's father had been injured, but not seriously. Jameel had a concussion, and so did Mumtaz. Shabanu had broken her arm in the automobile crash. Only Ibne had emerged without injury.

Thank God they would all be fine, Mumtaz thought, her mouth too sore to say anything at all. And then she fell back to sleep.

24

Shabanu sat beside Mumtaz as she drifted in and out of consciousness. When her daughter awoke, Shabanu leaned close to her ear and whispered, "I am here, daughter." She fed her broth and held a cup of water to her lips, fluffed her pillows, bathed her, and took her own meals sitting in the chair beside the bed.

By evening Mumtaz felt well enough to sit up. Shabanu arranged the pillows behind her daughter. She took a hair-brush and carefully brushed the tangles from Mumtaz's thick dark hair, then braided it into a single rope that fell down her back.

"I want to know everything," Mumtaz managed to say. Her tongue still ached, but the pain was duller now, and her words were slow but more intelligible.

Shabanu pulled her chair closer and took Mumtaz's hand in hers. She began by saying that Spin Gul had come to the haveli and cut the lock on the gate. He crept in to listen as

Samiya telephoned Ibne to say that he should meet them at the Multan train. He slapped Samiya to get her to tell him more, but she refused.

"Samiya is fine," Shabanu said quickly in answer to Mumtaz's raised eyebrows, and then went on. Spin Gul telephoned Nazir, whose airplane arrived in Multan before the train even pulled out of Lahore station.

"Omar and Tariq got to the haveli and caught Spin Gul and tied him up and called the police," Shabanu went on. Khoda Baksh stayed to keep watch over Spin Gul until the police came. Omar and Tariq climbed back into the car and sped off for Multan. They got there after the train, but there was only one road Ibne would have taken into the desert and they followed close behind. They arrived just a minute or so after the wreck, and almost crashed into the whole mess at the barrier. Omar was driving carefully because he expected something like the boulders.

"But how did Nazir know you were still alive?" asked Mumtaz. This had been on her mind ever since she saw Nazir raise his gun. She would never have forgiven herself if Nazir had hurt her mother because Mumtaz couldn't keep her secret!

Shabanu shook her head. "It was you and Jameel he was after," she said. "He thought he should be the tribal leader. He actually rubbed his eyes when he saw me, as if he were seeing a ghost." She smiled slightly.

"Will you stay here?" Mumtaz asked. There were so many things she needed to know to be able to imagine her own life.

"Nay, daughter," said Shabanu. "You and Jameel can live here in the haveli. I am going to Cholistan to be with my family and to teach women to read. I will visit often. You two will be safe here with Auntie Selma."

"I don't want to marry Jameel," said Mumtaz miserably. "He doesn't want to marry me. I want to come with you!"

Shabanu pressed her lips together and nodded. "Let me talk to Omar," she said. "If Jameel really is opposed to marrying you, I will take you with me to Cholistan."

Shabanu helped Mumtaz get up and held her with one arm as she wobbled to the bathroom and back. Mumtaz fell asleep again with Shabanu beside her.

* * *

Omar came later that night and pulled up a chair beside Shabanu at Mumtaz's bedside while she slept. They talked about the wreck and the shooting and how Mumtaz was feeling.

"And what about Leyla?" Shabanu asked. Omar said nothing. "She sent Spin Gul to spy on us and told Nazir where we were. He could have killed us, and she was partly responsible."

"Leyla wants Jaffar to be the Amirzai leader someday," Omar said slowly. "I don't believe she was intending to hurt anyone. She just wasn't thinking of the consequences."

"Leyla has hated me ever since I married Rahim," said Shabanu, keeping her voice level. "I don't believe she didn't mean to hurt us."

"I can promise you she will not try again," said Omar. "I'm sending her to live with her mother in the Cantonment. She will have nothing to do with the wedding arrangements. Jaffar will stay with me. It will be a severe punishment for her not to have Jaffar and me with her. If Jameel and Mumtaz want to live at Number 5 Anwar Road, that's their prerogative."

"Mumtaz says Jameel doesn't want to marry her," said Shabanu. "If that's so, I want her to come with me to Cholistan."

"Mumtaz must stay here," Omar said gently. "This has been an enormous shock to Jameel. He loves Mumtaz. I know he does. I'll talk to him."

"But they must decide for themselves!" said Shabanu.

"Nazir is gone. She and Jameel are safe. They are the hope of the Amirzai people."

"So! You would perpetuate this system of feudal grandees?" Shabanu asked sharply. "After all that it's taken from you, you won't allow these children to choose for themselves?"

"Mumtaz will have a good life," he said. "I'll see to it as long as I live. And Jameel will see to it as long as he lives."

"And can they stay here, in the haveli?" Shabanu asked. Omar thought for a moment.

"They can stay wherever they like," he said, "so long as they are not in the same house with Leyla."

"You are your Uncle Rahim," she said quietly. Then they were quiet.

"After all this time, we have nothing to say?" asked Omar.

"My heart has no words," said Shabanu. "And if it did, there would be no use saying them."

She asked Omar to sit with Mumtaz for a bit while she took a break. As soon as her mother was gone, Mumtaz opened her eyes.

"This time it was my turn to hear," she said, smiling at Omar. "Unlike my mother, I do not think freedom to do whatever you want is necessarily a good thing. But first I must know that Jameel wants to marry me."

* * *

Shabanu climbed the stairs to the roof and went straight to the pigeons' cage. She slipped inside and held up her hands, and several birds landed on them. She caressed them and pressed them to her lips one at a time, and took each out to the edge of the roof, releasing it as she had the first two, until they all were free.

25

That night Jameel went to his room at Number 5 Anwar Road. Apart from napping on the airplane, he had not slept since two nights before in San Francisco. His grandfather was still alive the last time he went to sleep, he thought with a jolt. He wondered whether this would keep happening—if every time he thought a new thought, it would be in the realization that life was going on without Baba in the world.

Jameel changed into his pajamas and sat down at the desk in the corner of the room. He took Baba's letter out and reread it. He was almost surprised that it said the same thing as when he'd first read it. He crumpled it and hurled it to the floor, then thought better and picked it up, smoothed it out, refolded it, and placed it back in the desk drawer.

He took a tablet of blue vellum paper from the desk and began a letter to Chloe. She deserved at least an explanation of what had happened, why she would never see him again. He wrote the date, then sat with the pen poised for several minutes and realized he'd never be able to make her understand. He put the paper and pen away and sat with his forehead resting on his hands.

There was a light tap at the door, and Uncle Omar stuck his head in.

"I saw your light was still on," he said. "May I?"

"Please," said Jameel, "come in." He stood and motioned to the easy chair in the corner beside his desk, but Omar didn't sit.

"I know this can't be easy for you," said Omar.

"When were you going to tell Mumtaz and me?" asked Jameel. "Or were you going to kidnap us and—"

"Please don't be so bitter," said Omar. "Jameel, you and Mumtaz will be good for each other. You've known each other all your lives, and you've always been close."

"Didn't it ever occur to anyone that we both had our own ideas about how we'd live our lives?" Jameel asked. The tears were very close to spilling out of his eyes, and perhaps he'd never be able to think of how they'd tricked Mumtaz and him without being angry.

"You know I understand," said Omar. "The same happened to me when I came back from America."

"So just because the same thing happened to you, does that make it right that I should never see my friends again, never go to college and study to be an engineer, and—"

"Who says you can't go to university?" said Omar. "There's no reason you and Mumtaz can't go to university together after you're married. We all thought Baba would live for a long time. He wanted you to go to Stanford just as he did. You always wanted to go to Stanford. You can both finish school here and go back to California if that's still what you want."

Jameel didn't answer. He tried to imagine himself and Muti married and going together back to California. How would his friends accept Mumtaz—as his wife? Even at eighteen, when they would be on their way to college? And sex. He couldn't go there yet. The conversation with his father would come soon enough.

But the idea of going together back to the United States to university certainly was not his image of how things were done in Pakistan. In his time-travel fantasies he thought of his family—particularly his grandfather—as being purely in the realm of the past. Baba had gone to Stanford University in California, but he came straight back to Lahore. He was already married to Grandmother—an arranged marriage when he was fifteen—and he ran the family farms until Uncle Rahim died, when he became tribal leader.

"But I never wanted to be tribal leader. Why did they skip your generation? It's not fair! I should have more time."

Omar paced, listening carefully to Jameel.

"Something happened that changed me," said Omar. "I fell in love. It was not someone I could ever marry. She was already married. I was about to be married—it was hopeless and completely out of the question. I knew it was the kind of love that ends only in tragedy, like Shah Jahan and Anarkali. It was a matter of life and death. And then she died. I knew I would never be happy. I would never love anyone in that way again. So I honored my father's wishes and married your Auntie Leyla."

"But you never became tribal leader! It should be your responsibility, not mine!"

"Jameel, the woman I loved died because of the same tradition of vendetta and family honor that killed her husband. I didn't want any part of it. It was the only time I ever refused my father or my duty. I promised to do anything else to help him—but I couldn't carry on that tradition."

"And now you want me to?" asked Jameel.

"You and Mumtaz are a new generation," Omar said. "Things must change if Pakistan is to survive. You must be educated and wise. It was what Baba wanted. It's just that things happened more quickly than we anticipated."

* * *

Jameel climbed into bed and pulled the sheet over himself after Omar left. He'd never thought of his uncle as someone who would fall in love so deeply. He was a cheerful man, someone who liked things to run smoothly and peacefully. Jameel would never have guessed he had suffered such a terrible tragedy as the loss of his one true love.

Jameel closed his eyes, but sleep refused to come. Scenes kept appearing in his head like flash cards: his face twisted in mute anger as he washed his grandfather's body in preparation for the funeral; Uncle Nazir flying from his feet like a puppet yanked from a stage; Mumtaz lying on the ground with blood pouring from her mouth; the golden halo of Chloe's hair as she sailed from the ramp on her skateboard.

26

The servants cleaned shattered crystal from the front hallway for days. Auntie Leyla was nowhere to be seen. Jameel's mother was looking after things. Jameel was glad not to have to see Leyla after what she'd done.

Jameel grew restless, and his father told him he must stay at Number 5 Anwar Road. He swam in the morning, and wanted to go to the haveli to see Mumtaz.

"She's in purdah," said his mother.

Jameel opened his mouth to speak, but didn't. Purdah. He was quick to anger since the accident, even though he tried to understand the need for doing things the Pakistani way—the old way. He was fighting so hard against the familiar feeling of being stuck between times and places. If he felt stuck in San Francisco, he realized, at least he could get unstuck—it was just a feeling in California. But here in Lahore the stuck-ness was a reality.

Or was it? He thought of Mumtaz as smart, having a right to speak her mind and to act on her wishes. Their relationship could be that way—who was to say it couldn't? Perhaps he could learn to see purdah—women being kept separate from men—as just a formality, a reminder of the good things of the past, when it served to protect privacy and dignity. In California he'd always felt uncomfortable with the exposed navels and more. Was purdah so bad by comparison?

His mother's voice jolted him out of his thoughts.

"I know, Beta," said Nargis, holding up her hand. "It's a very old custom. But when you've been living here for a while you'll be surprised at how normal it will feel. You have to take the good with the bad, and there is a lot more good in the old ways than you might be willing to admit right now. The Amirzai people will expect these customs to be observed."

"I want to see how Mumtaz is," said Jameel.

"She's fine, Beta. Your father is tending to her twice a day. Like you, she needs to rest, to recover from the concussion. But she is already up and about."

* * *

In the days that followed, wedding preparations began. Nargis bustled about, calling for flowers and food and extra servants, shamiana, thousands of little white lights, all of the accoutrements of a wedding. Furniture was rearranged. A new chandelier was brought from Karachi and hung in the front hall. The house was cleaned in every corner.

Jameel watched the preparations as if he were watching a television show. He thought of Chloe. He wanted to call her, at least to tell her what was about to happen. But he knew it would be incomprehensible to her. He grieved. He'd never again wonder at her golden hair and blue eyes. He'd never be Jimmy again. He wanted to see Mumtaz. He wondered whether she felt as trapped as he did.

Jameel's father made him sit in the front parlor with Uncle Omar each afternoon to receive tribesmen, to hear their complaints and solve their problems concerning land, crops, or family issues, as Grandfather had done, and his brother and father and grandfather before him. The tribesmen had heard about the coming wedding and came to pay their respects.

Jameel listened as one man presented a petition to get back a piece of land his cousin had seized. Uncle Omar signed a paper ordering the cousin to tear down the fences he'd built and give back the land.

A shepherd came to complain that a neighbor had stolen his sheep. Omar ordered the two men to appear together and sorted out why the neighbor was stealing the sheep. It turned out the neighbor had felt wronged when the other had dammed his irrigation canal.

One man said he'd paid a bride price and the woman married a man from the next village. Omar ordered the woman to repay the bride price.

Jameel wondered how his uncle knew who to believe and what was the best way of solving these problems.

Maulvi Inayatullah came to dinner one evening, and afterward Omar asked the maulvi and Jameel and his father to come into the study. Jameel thought perhaps Omar was going to tell him more about the plans that lay ahead. But instead the maulvi spoke.

"I know you think we imams are old-fashioned and backward," said Inayatullah, "but please listen." The old man spoke softly but urgently, and Jameel remembered the animated conversations Inayatullah and his grandfather had in this same study, one minute outshouting each other and the next dissolving into laughter. "You have only one family," Inayatullah went on. "If you were to turn your back on your people, you would cut yourself off from them. It will be as if you have no family at all. You can never replace them. That is a serious matter."

The maulvi paused, as if waiting for a response. Jameel said nothing, and he continued. "The second thing is that *mahabbat* here is very different from *love* in America. Here the word has to do with tradition, piety, duty, and family. When we talk of romance and passion, immediately we think of sadness or even tragedy. *Mahabbat* is a serious word."

"I don't care about cultural difference," said Jameel. "I want my life back."

"Maybe it was wrong that we didn't tell you before," said his father. "Your grandfather has always wanted you to be the tribal leader, since before you were born, even when Uncle Rahim was leader. Once your grandfather became leader he had the power to name his successor. Only he can change that determination. And he's no longer here to do that."

Jameel felt his anger rise again, and he was helpless to stop it.

"Why didn't you tell me? Why did you let me think I'd be like everyone else? That I'd grow up and make decisions for myself like other people do?" He felt the time warp engulf him again, as if he were stuck in medieval times.

"Your grandfather was strong and healthy, and we all thought he'd live to be a very old man. We wanted you to live like a normal boy for as long as possible."

"When will this marriage take place?" Jameel asked.

"It must be very soon," said Omar. "As we have already seen, trouble is inevitable when there is a void in leadership. After Mumtaz has recovered, you and she will marry. Perhaps within the week."

Three days passed as if he'd dreamed them. And then one afternoon Jameel found himself alone in the house. Even his mother had gone out to pick up the new waistcoat Omar had ordered for Jaffar.

He went to the intersection of Anwar and Canal Bank Road and hailed a motor rickshaw, ordering it to the walled city. He made his way to the haveli and pounded on the front gate.

Samiya and Shabanu were both on the other side of the gate when it swung open. They looked astonished to see him.

"I must see Mumtaz!" said Jameel. "I know we're not supposed to talk until the wedding, but I must!" Shabanu looked at him closely for a moment before nodding.

"Come with me," she said. They went up the back stairway to the rooftop, and Shabanu left him outside the pavilion. Mumtaz sat inside on the floor amid a pile of bolsters, still wearing white in honor of Baba's death.

Jameel felt as if he were seeing her for the first time. She looked lovely with her head bent over a piece of embroidery in her lap. Her long fingers were working over pale blue yarn on white cloth, and her graceful neck was arched as she concentrated. When Jameel saw the embroidery he grinned. It looked as if a small child had taken her first stitches, so long and uneven the pattern they made was unrecognizable. Muti looked up and saw his smirk.

"Hah!" she said. "You try it. I mean it. Come here and try doing this. You need six more hands!" Jameel went in and sat down beside her. He picked up the embroidery and tried. She was right: it was hard to hold and he stuck his finger with the first stitch. But even his first few stitches looked more respectable than hers.

Muti sniffed and sat back against a bolster, folding her arms.

"How's your tongue?" he asked.

"It's okay," she said. "Want to see?" She stuck out her tongue, which was still red and swollen.

"Eeuuw!" he said, and they both laughed.

"You do a better job than I do," said Mumtaz, nodding toward the piece of embroidery.

"Well, you know," said Jameel, "it just occurred to me: do you know we'll be wealthy after we marry? We can pay someone to do our embroidery and mending." Mumtaz smiled a small, sad smile.

"Uma says I can still go to Cholistan with her," Mumtaz said. "If you really don't want to get married, then I don't want to marry you, either. I don't want to lose you, Jameel. You've been my best friend all my life, and I don't want that to change."

Unexpectedly, a large lump formed in Jameel's throat. He nodded, and felt the sting of tears behind his eyes. "It won't," he said hoarsely. Then, for fear his tears would spill over, he stood and said, "I really have to get back. I just wanted to see how you are. My mother is watching over me like a hawk."

"Jameel," Muti said, and stood, too, "please just tell me. I'll go to Cholistan. They'll find someone more suitable for you to marry."

"Don't go to Cholistan," he said, his voice sounding more like a strange old man's voice. "I have to go." He turned and walked quickly out of the pavilion, down the stairs, through the courtyard, and out through the front gate.

He wished he had stayed. He wanted to talk to Muti more and to assure her. But what could he say? That he'd be a good husband? She knew how much he'd liked Chloe, and he didn't want to say anything that would sound false to Muti. He was still angry, but gradually he was growing used to the idea that he and Muti would marry. He simply had not untangled his feelings about it.

The next night he went to sleep thinking it was the last night he'd sleep alone. Tomorrow, he thought, and every night until he died he would share a bed with Muti, his wife. It didn't seem real.

In the middle of the night he awoke to see a flame hovering over his bed. It was so bright he could not see beyond it.

"Who's there?" he asked. His heart hammered, and he blinked to be sure his eyes were open. The light sped around the room, as if in search of something. "What do you want?" he asked. The light stood still when he spoke. He wasn't scared. He wished Muti was there, and wondered what she'd say to make the djinni go away.

Jameel reached across the bed for his nightlight and switched it on. The floating light disappeared. He remembered the maulvi said that the light shone brightest in the darkest darkness. He got out of bed, and on the table below where the light had hovered was a faded color photograph of a man and woman sitting side by side. Jameel examined it under the lampshade. It looked like a photograph of him and Mumtaz. He turned it over, and the date, August 27, 1958, was stamped on the back. "Jameel's wedding" was scrawled in faded ink under the date. He looked at the photo again. It was his grandparents' wedding. The date was fifty years ago tomorrow, when his grandfather was fifteen, exactly Jameel's age.

Jameel got back into bed and switched off the light. He lay uncovered on the warm sheets, staring into the darkness. In his grandfather's day, cousins married to keep property in the family. But the maulvi was right. The American ideal of romantic love had become a part of him and he didn't know how to rearrange his thinking.

He thought of Mumtaz and realized for the first time how

much he valued her intelligence, her inability to be anything but honest. He thought of her sense of fun, her curiosity, the clearness of her eyes, and suddenly skateboarding seemed like something he did when he was a child. His parents and Uncle Omar knew how important the things were that he valued in Mumtaz.

"You and Mumtaz are a good match," said a voice beside the head of Jameel's bed. He turned to see Baba sitting beside the table. A faint white light and a sweetish whiff of betel nut emanated from him. Jameel raised himself to his elbows. "I felt the same way you're feeling before I married your grandmother," Grandfather went on. "And yet your grandmother and I were very happy until her death."

"Baba," Jameel said, "I had so many things planned . . ."

"And you needn't give them all up," said Grandfather. "Your Uncle Omar can handle things here while you and Mumtaz are at university. The experience of living in America will be good for her. It will be good for the two of you to live there together."

"But, Grandfather, in America . . ."

"You are not an American, Jameel," he said. "You may have a U.S. passport, but you have the blood of many generations of Amirzai leadership in your veins. You belong here."

"What do I have to offer?" Jameel asked miserably, and his grandfather laughed.

"Just what we need right now is what you offer," said his grandfather. "You honor Islam and you can help make Pakistan a more modern country. You and Mumtaz are strong and clever. You are ancient souls with modern eyes." Grandfather's form began to fade.

"Wait!" said Jameel. "I want you to tell me—about the djinn. And I want to know what it's like where you are. Wait!" There was no answer as his grandfather's form faded to an almost invisible outline. "Please, Baba," he said, "I haven't even said goodbye!" But the figure disappeared completely. Jameel stared into the darkness, and he knew that the djinni had done its job. His grandfather was right. This was his place, and he knew now what to tell Mumtaz.

GLOSSARY

(Pronunciation guide: accented syllable is italicized; *ah* = vowel sound in *call*; *eh* = vowel sound in *check*; *ih* = vowel sound in *chick*; *oh* = vowel sound in *dough*; *uh* = vowel sound in *stuff*; *ai* = vowel sound in *try*; *oo* = vowel sound in *true*; *ooh* = vowel sound in *hoof*; *ee* = vowel sound in *tea*.)

Ah-salaam-aleikum (ah-sah-*lahm*-ah-*leh*-koom)—Peace be upon you

aloo paratha (ah-*loo* pah-*rahn*-tah)—fried bread containing onion and potato

amrud (ahm-*rood*)—guava, a yellow, pearlike fruit

annee-jannee (*ah*-nee-*jah*-nee)—coming and going

atta (*ah*-tuh)—ground whole-grain wheat

ayah (*aiy*-uh)—nursemaid or maid

Baba (*bah*-buh)—Father or Grandfather

Basant (*buh*-sahnt)—spring festival

beta (*beh*-tah)—son

bhoondi ladoo (*boohn*-dee *lah*-doo)—small cakes with raisins and nuts

biryani (beer-*yah*-nee)—rice cooked with vegetables and/or meat

bukri (*buh*-kree)—goat

burfi (*buhr*-fee)—a sweet dish made by boiling milk until it is the consistency of paste

burqa (*bhur*-kuh)—a traditional head-to-toe covering worn by Islamic women with a lattice of cloth in front of the eyes to allow vision

chador (*chah*-door)—also a traditional head covering, usually an untailored cloth draped about the head and body

chai (chaiy)—tea

channa (*chuhn*-nuh)—chickpeas

chappal (*chuhp*-puhl)—sandal

charpoi (*chahr*-poy)—a string cot

chawal (*chuh*-vuhl)—rice

choti (*choh*-tee)—little

chowkidar (*choh*-kee-dahr)—a watchman who stands beside a gate

churidar (*choor*-ee-dahr)—bias-cut pants with drawstring waist

dahi (*dah*-hee)—yogurt

darzi (*duhr*-zee)—tailor

desi (*deh*-shee)—country, rural

dhobi (*dhoh*-bee)—washerman

dhurrie (*dhuh*-ree)—a flat woven rug with no pile

djinni (*jihn*-ee) (pl: djinn)—a mischievous spirit that can take the shape of a human or a light; its purpose is to teach a lesson

dupatta (doo-*pah*-tuh)—a long scarf worn loosely over the head

durbar (*duhr*-buhr)—room where a leader receives followers and official guests

eek, do, teen (ehk, doh, teen)—one, two, three

gaay (gaiy)—cow

halwa (*hahl*-vuh)—dessert dish made with milk and often carrot

haveli (hah-*veh*-lee)—a private house traditionally with court yard, often owned by a wealthy family in a city

jalabi (juh-*leh*-bee)—a pretzel-shaped, deep-fried sweet

Janazah (juh-*nuh*-zuh) (Arabic)—prayer asking forgiveness for the dead

kameez (kuh-*meez*)—a knee-length tunic worn over loose-fitting trousers

khansama (khan-*sahm*-muh)—cook

kheer (keer)—pudding made with either rice or vermicelli

lungi (*loohn*-gee)—a piece of cloth worn around the hips

mahabbat (mah-*hah*-baht)—love

maidan (*maiy*-dahn)—an open space, often a small park in the center of a neighborhood

mali (*mah*-lee)—gardener

Masha' Allah (mah-*shah*-luh)—God's will

maulvi (*mohl*-vee)—a learned Islamic scholar, usually regarded as a holy man

nimbu pani (*nihm*-boo *pah*-nee)—a drink made with nimbu, a small lime, and pani, water, with either sugar or salt

nimbu soda (*nihm*-boo *soh*-dah)—a drink made with nimbu, a small lime, and club soda, with either sugar or salt

pakshi (*pahk*-shee)—bird

paratha (pah-*rahn*-tah)—fried unleavened bread

purdah (*puhr*-dah)—literally, a curtain; the practice of keeping women separate and out of sight of men

rasmali (rahs-muhl-*aiy*)—a pudding made with red carrots

rickshaw (*rihk*-shah)—here, the three-wheeled taxi in most Indian and Pakistani cities

roti (*roh*-tee)—bread

rupee (*roo*-pee)—Pakistani currency

salaams (sah-*lahms*)—greetings

sardar (sahr-*dahr*)—title used by Pakistani and Afghan tribal leaders

shalwar (*shahl*-wahr)—loose-fitting trousers with a drawstring waist

shalwar kameez (*shahl*-wahr kuh-*meez*)—traditional Punjabi dress for men and women: a long tunic worn over loose-fitting trousers with drawstring waist

shamiana (*shah*-mee-*yah*-nuh)—a large tent made of colored cloth sewn together in geometric patterns

shatoosh (shah-*toosh*)—a fine shawl made from the finest chin and belly hairs of wild Himalayan goats

Swati chair (*swah*-tee chair)—a low wooden chair from the Valley of Swat in northern Pakistan

Uma (ooh-mah)—Mother

wallah (*wahl*-luh)—a purveyor, one who sells a product or service

Zamzam (zahm-zahm)—water from the mosque at the Islamic holy city of Mecca

Suzanne Fisher Staples is an award-winning author whose novels for young adults include *Shabanu* and *Haveli,* companion novels to *The House of Djinn.* Before writing books, she worked for many years as a UPI correspondent in Asia, with stints in Pakistan, Afghanistan, and India. She currently resides in Nicholson, Pennsylvania.